GODS WILL
BUT MY CHOICE

Uncut Raw Christian Fiction

by Timm Knight

VISIT www.timmknight.com To see video & hear music from Timm
Knight inspired from Gods Will But My Choice! Get details on the
Kindle HD 6 Giveaway /Join the mailing list/ Share with your
friends/blogs/facebook/twitter Leave feedback on Amazon!

Table of Contents

THE BATTLE BEGINS

It's June 18, 1995, a 14-year-old boy named Tim Stewart, decided it was time to start his own gang. The now, mostly rundown city of Clarksville needed another gang like it needed another pothole in the street. Fortunately, his idea of establishing himself as a self-appointed leader, did not include violence nor crime as a prerequisite for membership. Their primary focus would be on coming up with legal ways and means to get money in the streets. Once his team was in order, the first goal would be to get some wheels. Undoubtedly, he was too young to drive a car but just old enough to get a street bike from Avis's bike shop. He figured standard bicycles were all too common for a young man of his status, besides, everyone had one. He wanted to be anything but ordinary, so everything he does has to make a statement. Even though, Clarksville was considered "the hood" there was a two block stretch that was considered decent or the "safe side" of the town. The 1500 block of Grand Ave is where the supposed safe side began, with Tim living smack dab in the middle of the block. Tim was admittedly very privileged and unapologetically happy about his lot in life thus far, from a financial standpoint at least. This fact made him very popular amongst the ladies yet the focal point of immeasurable hate from his male counterparts. Knowing this, he was very aware his selection process for friends/gang members had to be thorough to avoid getting set up within his camp. Tim is tall and slender with an athletic build, boasting a 2 inch high top fade with a slanted part in it. He always had on the hottest gear, Karl Kani, Gucci, Polo, Louis Vuitton you name it, and it was guaranteed to be in his closet. Jordans in almost every color to match his outfits, which he never wore twice. And of course he had to have the smell goods on, before school he would spritz himself with Joop cologne. To complete his look he worn a thick gold herringbone chain like Tupac in the music video "I get around". Now, after much deliberation he recruited his first three members, Rick Jones, Tamir Pryor & Marshall Edwards. Rick & Marshall lived alongside Tim on the "good" side of town. Both boys benefited from having two hard working class parents. Tamir, however, lived with his grandma on Reading Street five blocks over. Even though Tamir had the least amount of money, he was the master at making the most of what he did have, he was the ultimate hustler. Keeping with his original idea, there were no crazy rituals, jump in's or random shootings necessary. In fact, they've known each other for years, so a brief discreet, individual conversation was all that was needed solidify their bond. Image is everything in Clarksville as it is in any other hood. There are they haves, and the have-nots and those mad about whatever you got. With this in mind, Tim would periodically loan out clothes and shoes to his new recruits to help keep up appearances, especially on the weekends. Now that everyone was on one accord they would often gather at their official headquarters, Tim's front yard. Primarily, they would just hang out, laugh and talk for hours about the good times that were ahead. That momentous day when they would be able to show off their brand new Kawasaki dirt bikes. They talked about speeding down the block poppin' wheelies, doing circles and without question burning plenty of rubber in the street. With the vision firmly cemented in their minds eye, they agreed there was no compromising and no turning back. They even found the ideal location to learn and perfect new tricks, the back of Clark's supermarket. About two years ago new construction began to add an addition onto Clark's supermarket. However, due to a lack of funds the project was scrapped, and all that was left was mounds of dirt. Fast forward, it's now the last day before the much-anticipated summer vacation. Tim, Rick, Tamir, and Marshall are at Clark High school in their homeroom hallway before class. They lean their backs against the lockers, with one foot on the ground while the base of the other foot is against the locker. Feeling like ghetto celebrities they embrace the love and attention from the young ladies passing by smiling. At this point, their arms are folded, as their eyes look through knock-off Versace glasses at students on their way to their respective homerooms. In this section of the hallway, sunlight beams in from the window directly on their lockers making them squint their eyes, hence the shades. Now, to the teachers it appeared that these boys must've been vitamin D deficient or just really enjoyed basking in the sun every morning. However, both assumptions were wrong. The truth of the matter is that they endured the direct exposure to the sunlight so everyone could see they had it going on. Then, like clockwork the school bell rings signaling it was the start of the first period. Tim stomps his blue and red Nike's down hard as he could, making sure to get the attention of his friends. They remained lined up against the locker, he walks by them slowly as if he were a military drill sergeant. "Meet me at my house after school I have a major announcement. Also, I need ya'll to be at Ms. Folsom's class soon as yours lets out!" He says in a stern voice. In the past, the last day of school always arrived with its own preset agenda. If you had a problem with someone or if someone had a problem with you. Rest assured, the last day of school was when the score would be settled, as there were no worries of getting suspended. As it stood, Tim lived somewhat of a double life. In class, he was a straight A student though he would never admit this to his friends for the sake of not being seen as cool. At the same time, he displayed thug tendencies frequently getting into fights in the neighborhood. He had been having issues with a kid named Darius, who lived on the east side of Clarksville, which was about 10 miles from the West side where Tim lived. In reality, the chances of them meeting in the street were slim to none. But there had been rumors that Darius wanted to put hands and feet on him for talking to Stacy Johnson, who was new to the school. Darius knew in his heart of hearts that he was truly God's gift to ladies. With this thought etched in his mind, he believed he should have the first chance to rap to every beautiful girl, before anyone else. However, Tim was not informed or concerned about Darius's warped rules of entitlement. He approached Stacy one day while walking past her house on the way to the park. After a little small talk, he was successful getting her number on the first try. From there they began hanging out on a regular basis, so much so she could have been a considered an honorary member of the crew. Naturally, Darius was furious when he found out about this but couldn't do anything about it. Not surprisingly, he had been suspended numerous times throughout the year for bullying and terrorizing students. In light of this, he faced juvenile detention if he got in trouble again. All things considered, it was highly unlikely the day would end without some sort of fireworks display, taking place in June instead of July. The half day of school had zoomed by, students are freely walking down the halls back to their homerooms for the last time awaiting dismissal into summer bliss. Tim and Rick share the same homeroom and are sitting at their desk in the back of Mrs. Folsom's' history class. Mrs. Folsom was a tall, slender, soft-spoken African American teacher who could've been a model in a magazine. She closes her notebook rises from her desk and sits on the edge of the desk with legs carefully crossed. "Class, before you go for the summer, study those packets I have given you, please! And Remember, everything you do to make a better you, makes a better you! Lastly guys, try to do something positive this summer and stay out of trouble" she said. The back of Tim and Ricks' desk faced the back of the windows which were wide open. Tim could feel the hot air blowing on his back like a heater, as it was close to 99 degrees that day. He could also feel the tension mounting as he looked closely at the clock, the extended hand was fast approaching the 12, lining up correctly with the shorthand already on 12. He is slowly allowing his mind to accept the reality that he's about to be released into a potentially dangerous situation. Rick, who sits directly across from him, looks at Tim and says "Hey man, you okay? You look like you're zoning out over there". Tim was looking extremely focused on the back of Kevin's fat round shaped head with creases in it who was seated in front of him. Tim breaks his concentration and replies. "Naw, man I'm fine, I'm just calculating how many times I'm gonna bust Darius upside his head if he comes at me today" followed by a somewhat nervous laugh. It's important to note that Darius was known for fighting dirty, Tim wasn't sure if he would have a weapon on him or not. Gone were the days Tim's dad talked about when men settled their issues with only their fist so both men could live to see another day. In Clarksville, the youth didn't seem too concerned with whether they lived or died much less anyone else's welfare. Finally, the extended hand hit the 12 and it was now time to deal with whatever was to come. Tim had no books to carry, so he gets up turns to look out the window, closes his eyes, and takes a deep breath as he prepared to go to battle. Tim was the self-appointed leader of his crew, he recognized any sign of weakness could jeopardize his leadership. The Class is dismissed, then all at once, students from around the school start rushing into the green colored hallway with matching lockers. It was as if they were given advanced notice that something was about to go down. Meanwhile, Rick and Tim are the last to exit the room. "Let's get to my locker ASAP where the rest of the fellas will be," Tim says. But no sooner did the words leave his mouth did his nose press directly into the chest of Darius, who was right at the front door. He stood 6'2 and weighed 200lbs of shear muscle. From Rick's perspective, it appeared as if the entire school came alongside Darius. "Now what you gonna do punk? I heard you talking to Stacy?" said Darius. Tim quickly glanced up while removing his nose from the logo on Darius's shirt that read "Do Somethin". Tim's first thought in his mind was that his hour had come, like when they came in the night to capture Jesus. Ready or not it was about to go down. What he did not see though, was that the school security team was running the same direction as all the other kids, who were coming from the other hallways to see the fight. Darius wasted no time and swings on Tim, but thanks to quick reflexes Tim ducks down. He comes back up with a powerful uppercut that connects right to Darius's mouth. Darius, who seemed unfazed by the punch that bloodied his mouth cocks back to throw a hard right hand but his arm, is caught mid throw by the school officer. "Hey! Hold it right there Darius!" Officer Stroud yelled. "I just knew you were gonna start some trouble today, I knew it." Darius struggles with Officer Stroud to regain freedom of his arm, they were both the same height and seemed to be equally matched strength wise. Darius was trying to get to Tim with all his might, but backup security had already gotten there and started to restrain him knocking him to the ground. "You think this is over! Exclaimed Darius. "Nobody puts their hands on me and lives, you hear me?" he shouted as security was bringing him back up to his feet. By this time, Tamir and Marshall had joined Tim and Rick. For the moment, Tim is feeling extremely relieved inside that things ended like they did, but acted like he was ready for war in front of his crew and the many onlookers. "Do I look like I'm scared?" forging toward Darius as his friends were holding him back and the officers began walking Darius in the opposite direction. At this point, Tim and the crew headed for double doors leading to the school front steps. Tim forcefully pushes the doors open catching an immediate blast of the 99-degree heat coupled with what seemed like the brightest sunshine ever witnessed. The air was hot and muggy so Tim immediately took off his T-shirt, threw it over his shoulder just then he noticed a crowd of kids swarming around them like bees. One onlooker yells "It's about time somebody put Darius in his place!" Tim looked at the boy, smirked "Yeah, you're right." Tim knew that 10 miles would not be a great enough distance to keep him from coming face to chest again with a vengeance-seeking Darius. Never had Darius been embarrassed like this in front of the whole school. Tim knew his small battle victory just started a war. "Hey fellas, just come by the house in the morning around 10 for the meeting I was talking about." They nodded their head in agreement and went their separate ways.

TWOS A CROWD

The first official school free day has arrived for Tim. He slowly wakes up on his own without the annoying beeping sound of his alarm clock. "What a relief," he says to himself as he throws off the blue sheet that he was covered under from head to toe. He sits up on the bed, slowly turns to his left, still seated, plants his feet firmly on the ground listening for signs of life beyond his closed door. There is just a little bit of sunlight peeking through the white blinds on his window, illuminating his collection of posters of his favorite rappers and singers. The once blue walls were now almost completely covered with posters that are evenly spaced and neat. His room is spacious and surprisingly clean for a teenage boy, his room is always organized and in order. Tim is extremely fussy about almost everything to let his friends tell it. For example, his clothes, shoes, and hats have to be organized in his closet in a precise order that never changes. His video games are lined up perfectly against the wall next to his 50-inch projection screen TV, in the 90's this was a big deal. Tim was rather fortunate in terms of having nice things unlike many of his friends. However, he had no clue as to the financial hardship that had been silently plaguing his mom and dad. Primarily the weight of this financial burden was on his father, Robinson. His mother Sunny is actually his stepmother through remarriage to Robinson. Sunny never really took a liking to Tim, it was thought that because she lost her only son Tyrone in a car accident 3 years prior, she was jealous of the bond between Tim and Robinson. Sunny and her previous husband, Rich got divorced, he has since moved on with a new marriage and had another boy. Meanwhile, Sunny finds out after much trying that she can no longer have children a year into her 2-year relationship with Robinson. Robinson and Sunny only dated for a couple months before deciding to move forward into both of their second marriages. Tim noticed her aloofness early on and mentioned how this made him feel to his dad. Robinson brushed it off as Tim simply not accepting her due to the break up with his mother. One thing was certain Robinson was not receptive to the idea of allowing a then 11-year-old to hinder his chances for a new relationship. Robinson never explained what happened to him and Tim's mom Loretta marriage. All Tim knew was that after the divorce, his mom moved to Arizona with his sister Keyana and had not sent for or contacted him since her departure. It was clear to Tim along with many other family members who encountered Sunny, that Robinson was lonely and wanted companionship. Ironically, Sunny did not live up to her names definition by any means. She was extremely pessimistic, always focused on anything negative, she was always full of gossip. Sunny has dark skin along with a rather large frame and feet. She wore a size 11 and a half in women's shoes. Her hair was always kept in cornrows, but she would never be seen in public without wearing a bleach blonde wig that would hang down her back. You could always hear her loud conversations while seated in her favorite spot. She could usually be found stretched out in the living room on the pink and white cloth couch on the phone with her girlfriend, Patty. "Girl did you hear this? Girl did you hear that?" a typical intro to any conversation from Sunny. When she did manage to tear the phone away from her ear to talk to Robinson, it was always the same exchange like a broken record. If she wasn't giving all the details on a forthcoming deadly storm, it would be what car the Davis's just bought and why they don't need it. Down to who got shot in the neighborhood or just complaining about something as simple as a single fork being left on the kitchen counter. You could rest assured something negative was going to come out of her lips which were usually covered with a bright orange lipstick color. Sunny spoke very little to Tim if at all. Any issues concerning him and there were many in her estimation, would go directly to Robinson immediately upon opening the door after returning home from work. It was like she got a kick out of trying to bring a wedge in between their relationship. Somehow, Robinson was usually able to defuse her cataclysmic concerns diplomatically. So Tim, pretty much ignored her as if she didn't exist. Tim was typically very mild mannered until provoked and Sunny knew exactly what buttons to push to get him angry. One thing, in particular, is not respecting Tim's privacy. Though only 14 he considered himself very much a man in many ways. She learned early on that he was great at ignoring her, but invading his space would always get a response out of him. Tim's room was one of the two bedrooms downstairs, his parents' room was upstairs. Oddly enough, even though the house was over 35 years old, the green plush covered carpeted steps did not creek going up or down. Sunny throws on her over worn cream house robe comes down to the stairs, burst open Tim's door without a knock or concern for privacy. "Tim, I heard you were up at the school fighting like a knucklehead," she said with anger in her voice. "Sunny!" Tim yelled in frustration. "Why are you opening my door? You know you're supposed to knock before you come in here!" he says bitterly. "Who are you yelling at little boy? See, this is the attitude that got you in trouble the other day. I heard about your fighting in school and I can't wait to tell your father, you little devil" she says in a childlike manner. Tim doesn't respond turns his back and continues to search through his top dresser drawer for a t-shirt, underwear and socks before the door so rudely swung open. "You know you hear me boy, what are you deaf?". Annoyed at being ignored, she goes over to the dresser where he's gathering his things together, she rests one hand on her hip and the other on the edge of the top part of the drawer. "I don't know who you think you are ignoring me" moving nose to nose with Tim. He rolls his eyes and breathes out hard holding his underwear, socks and t-shirt in one hand. Then slams the top drawer with all his might with an attitude as he looks at her in the eye. He did not realize her fingers were hanging over the edge, the impact of the slam broke two of her five fingers. "Owwwwww" she let out an irking scream and began to tear up. "Ohhhh I could just...." but stops herself mid-sentence. "Your dad is gonna throw you out of here for abusing me like this" she shouted. Tim smirked, "Well that should teach you to keep out of my room and my drawers!" Tim knew that comment would only add fuel to a fire that would soon be engulfed in flames. But he figured since he never talked back to her before, today would be a good day to start as he knew the situation could get no worse especially after she talks to his dad.

HERE WE GO

After taking his shower, Tim walks back down the hall toward his room to get dressed. However, this time once inside his room, he makes sure his door is locked behind him. He opens his closet door to what appeared as a sea of clothes along with various assortment of pants and shirts. Once dressed, he made his way into the kitchen to find Sunny sitting at the circular glass table with her head cocked to the side of her shoulder as the phone pressed against her left ear. "Patty, are you on your way?" She said without acknowledging Tim's presence in the room. She had previously told Patty all about what happened earlier and as a consequence was in too much pain to drive herself to the hospital. Tim went to the cabinet, pulled out a bowl, then reaches for the only cereal that was left Honey Bunches of Oats. Ironically, just as fast as his hand reached for the box Sunny darts up from the table with cat like reflexes to snatch the box away from him. "That's MY cereal and you can't have none!" she exclaimed. Like usual he ignored her completely but threw the glass bowl into the sink so hard it shattered, shards of glass were everywhere. At that point he just calmly walks out onto the porch as if nothing happened. Up to the present time, Tim had purposely kept one chair on the top of the concrete steps for him to sit on. Leaving guest no choice but to sit on one of the four steps below him when they visited. The front lawn was always kept neat, the steps were surrounded by two gigantic shrubs which came up a little above his waist when standing. It often doubled as a mini fortress while sitting down. No sooner than he sat down in his chair, did he noticed his crew making their way up the block toward his house. He was rather pleased to see his friends approaching and yells "Hey, ya'll right on time". They gather around, Rick leans his arm on the railing which is virtually swallowed up by the shrubs. Tamir takes a seat on the third step and Marshall just stands in the front facing Tim. "You good? Why is your face all frowned up?" Rick says, anticipating there might be a problem. "I can't take no more of her crap man! She has it out for me, first I had to deal with Darius, now I gotta deal with her, which also means I gotta deal with my dad. And to make matters worse, I'm pretty sure I broke two of her fingers by mistake" Tim says while stretching his arms up then connecting his fingers together placing them behind his head. After a minute, he stares up at the sky as if the answers to life's questions were going to magically be bestowed upon him. Looking at him dumbfounded Marshall is first to respond "You broke Sunny's fingers?"Tamir chimes in "Yo, that's crazy! I guess she only needs one finger to dial 911 so she should be good" he laughs. Tamir was the jokester of the crew, to him everything was funny. "You ain't right Tamir," Rick said in a semi-serious tone then says. "No, seriously what happened T." Tim takes a look back at the screen door to make sure it was closed before speaking. "We'll, like usual, I'm in my room mind my business, then out of nowhere she just barges in, talking bout what she heard at school. Mainly looking for a reason to get under my skin. I'm totally not paying her any attention when she comes over and rest her fingers on my top drawer. Long story short after I got my underwear I was mad so I slammed the drawer and it's snap, crackle pop. I'm like that's what you get" he says while shrugging his shoulders. Rick with an even more confused look on his face says "Are you serious?" looking directly into Tim's face seeing the coldness in his eyes. "Yeah, why would I lie?" Tim said nonchalantly. But before he could go into any further details, a brand new white 1995 Mercedes S 550 with all tinted windows pulls up. The driver was honking the horn repeatedly like a lunatic. "Yo Tim, who in the world is honking the horn like that?" Tamir asks as all of their eyes are glued to the driver side of the car. All of a sudden, Sunny opens the front and screen doors, then charges ahead "Move out my way boy" she says to Tim as she purposely bumps his chair with the screen door. "Ya'll move too, always sitting on my steps. Don't ya'll have a home?" Sunny says with her nose wrinkled up as she moves swiftly down the four steps. Patty puts the window down and yells as Sunny is walking toward the car "Girl, why you allow all these hoodlums to be in front of your house like this? This is exactly why I don't come over here. These boys ain't up to no good". Sunny walks around to the passenger side of the car, Patty takes off her seat belt, reaches over her seat to open the door from the inside. "Get in, I got to see your fingers girl" Sunny flops her butt down into the soft white leather seats and puts her purse on the floor. Blown away after seeing the damaged fingers Patty says, "Oh my god! Sunny, those fingers are definitely broke girl! You should've tried to break his neck with your good hand!" Patty is shaking her head, disgusted by the situation, she puts her seat belt back on and proceeds backing out the driveway. "Look, all I'm saying is that if it were me, I would've killed that boy" looking back over at Sunny's limp fingers. Sunny is becoming even more enraged now that Patty is bringing even more attention to it "Yeah, you know I should've, but I want to see his dad finally punish him for something. He never got with him the whole time I have known him and it makes me sick. Robinson swears Tim can do no wrong, but now he's gonna see he's not the angel he thinks he is. And get this, he threw a glass bowl at me, got glass all over the floor girl" Sunny says looking out the window. "If he doesn't beat him down for this you'd be a fool to stay any longer!" proclaimed Patty as she drives recklessly down the street headed for the hospital. She looks over at Sunny making sure to make eye contact. "And don't forget my nephews don't live that far from here. I can have them reach out and touch both of these losers if need be." Patty says rolling her neck from left to right "Listen, you deserve better than to be dealing with Robinsons' money issues and being disrespected by his son at the same time".

THE PLAN

"Anyways," Tim says releasing a deep breath, then all at once appearing as if he was totally unaffected by the recent developments. "Listen up guys, by the end of the summer we're gonna have brand new bikes to floss around in" he affirmed. "It's time to stop talking about it and finally being about it" as he looked over at his BMX bike leaning against his red colored brick house. "In fact, some of you have walked long enough! Now the time has come to graduate into the big leagues" he said while rubbing his hands together like an evil villain who came up with a sinister plan to destroy the world. He stood up on his front porch speaking boldly and proud as if he was the president of the United States, making a speech to a crowd of thousands. In reality, it is just three people. Rick, Tamir, and Marshall. As Tim stepped down from his imaginary throne, he greeted the fellas with their special handshake. The shake was a combination of a few up and down slaps followed by a few from side to side. "So that's all we gonna focus on going forward, got it?" he said making eye contact with each of the boys individually. The boys were seemingly in agreement, however, as Tim heads into the backyard, Rick whispers to Marshall as they began to follow him into the back. "This guy is crazy, there's no way we're gonna get those bikes before the end of summer, fall or winter for that matter." Marshall looks at Rick puzzled by his statement "Why you say that? I mean, if he said it, then he must have a plan to get the money. Anyway, if that's how you feel, why not tell him?" Rick, extremely annoyed at Marshall for not responding back in a low tone, begins backpedaling. "No, I'm just saying, well, look never mind, just forget it," he says in a low voice, hoping to bring the sidebar conversation to an abrupt end. Everyone is now in the backyard as Tim enters in the small white garage that his dad primarily kept his tools in. He waves them inside and over to a dust covered steel cabinet, he opens the top drawer and grabs out four pieces of paper. Tim hands out three of the four brochures faced down and returns back in front of the cabinet with one in hand for the briefing. "Okay fellas, you can turn your papers over. At this moment, you're holding the game changer for us all! Ain't nobody, this side of Clarksville, got these here" he says smiling from ear to ear. "Now if you look over to the right" extending his right hand, pointing in the direction of four buckets. "These my friends, hold all the money we need to pay for our bikes," he says with excitement in his voice. Every gang has to have a leader and as stated earlier Tim, was the self-appointed leader of the crew. It made perfect sense in many ways because he always had money not to mention he was skilled with the gift of persuasion. In Tim's mind at 14 years old there were two necessities every teen must have. One is the ability to buy whatever you want, be it the newest beeper, video game, finest sneakers and clothes at will without waiting for your parents. And the second thing which to some may sound odd but a big deal for him. The ability to buy his favorite ice cream, strawberry éclairs from the ice cream truck whenever it rolled through the neighborhood. Clarksville was a relatively large suburb of New Franklin with many sections of it. Even still, the ice cream truck would go through the Clarksville Heights section practically every hour on the hour so by day's end, Tim would have usually scarfed down at least three or four éclairs. Watching his dad count wads of cash before storing in his safe deposit box inspired Tim to get money of his own. The houses over in Clark Heights are huge and back in their heyday were some of the most desirable in all the city. Grand Ave, where Tim lives, is all but completely run down, however there we still a few standout properties and his house was included in that number. Now for most 14-year-old boys having all the latest games and technology would have been enough, but Tim wanted to look good in all areas of his young life. At this point, his primary concern is to impress his friends, onlookers and most importantly grow his organization. Getting these bikes would strengthen his image as a boss in the neighborhood. He slowly walks over to the window where the buckets are lined up, the boys follow him attentively with their eyes. He then bends down, grabs a bucket and carries it over to Tamir. "Now look in the bucket, you each got soap, a sponge, turtle wax, a towel and terry cloth. All you need to be in business, we'll, shall I say my business" He says while clearing his throat. "I'm extending to you an opportunity to be what we entrepreneurs call a franchise owner" with an optimistic expression on his face. "Are you serious? I'm not down for washing a million cars for chump change! How many cars you gotta wash to make any kinda money anyway?" Says Tamir completely dismissing the idea as he walks toward the front of the garage which is still open. Marshall looks at Tim's face, which is starting to frown up as he goes over to Tamir and says. "Look negro, a little hard work ain't never hurt nobody and looking at your sneaks, you should've been working," Tim interjects "Exactly, where do you guys think I get the money for all the games, beepers, shoes, clothes and everything else I got?" Rick, who was just looking around in the garage, says, "Hmm, I don't know, your dad?" Tim shakes his head "No, not at all! About three years ago I asked him for some Jordans that were $150. He said he wasn't gonna spend $150 on no sneakers, but he could show me how I could earn them. So of course I was curious, he took me to his car lot and showed me the difference between washing cars and detailing. And believe me, there's a big difference, but I got those Jordans, so in the end it was all worth it. After a while, you forget about how hard it is and focus on the rewards. And that's how I'm able to get whatever I want." Marshall, taking it all in "Ok, that explains it, I just thought your dad was loaded and you were spoiled" laughing. Tamir walks out of the garage into the backyard picks up a basketball, raises his arm with the ball in the palm of his hand releases it straight into the basketball hoop. "Well, with a J like this! I'm destined for the NBA" smirks

Tamir."I never knew that's how you got stuff, I thought your sister moving away had become the best thing that ever happened to you". Shrugging his shoulders clearly being condescending, he puts up another jump shot. Tim enraged runs out the garage leading with what looked like flying fists of fury towards Tamir only to be cut short by Rick and Marshall leaping into the line of fire. "Hey, relax, what did I say?" Tamir says looking like a deer caught in headlights. Tim is practically about to break free of the boys grasp. "Look, I was just saying I thought her leaving was the reason you were getting all that stuff," Tamir said with a half-hearted look of concern on his face. "You black guys are so quick to fight somebody, whoops wait, I guess I'm black too," he says playfully trying to lighten the mood to no avail. "You really don't know when to shut your mouth, do you?" Marshall said while still struggling to keep Tim back. "Say another word and I'm gonna let you guys go at it." Just as Marshall said those words, Tim broke free and came nose to nose with Tamir and slaps the ball he was holding out of his hand with all his might. "Whoa, whoa dude relax!" Tamir said backing away. "Yeah that's right, you better back down," Tim said as if he had just taken the heart right out of Tamir's' chest. "Keep my sisters name out your mouth period or I will knock you out punk" Rick and Marshall quickly regain custody of Tim, but he pushes their arms away forcefully. "Get off me! I ain't gonna touch him". Tim walks over to the back steps that lead to the back entrance of the house and sits down. "Ya'll really crack me up. I show ya'll a legit way to get some paper and ya'll don't seem the least bit interested. And this comedian over here is about to lose his whole front row of teeth thinking he's funny". Rick and Marshall follow Tim over to the back steps, while Tamir goes over by the fence to recover the basketball that went flying minutes before and starts shooting around again. Tim storms into the house without notification to the others, into the kitchen, grabs three Snickers bars out the cabinet. Meanwhile Rick, Marshall, and Tamir are still outside talking. "Yo, your stupid Tamir, Why would you bring up his sister?

You know how he feels about that situation" Marshall said, looking over the fence at Mr. Barker's pear tree debating if he wanted to go grab one. "Jordan," Tamir says as he makes a three pointer while leaving his hand in the air and sticking his tongue out. "Man, I was just saying what everybody has been thinking. Rick I'm sure you thought the same thing so don't even act like I'm the only one" Tamir says adamantly as he returns to his solo game of basketball. Tim opens the screen door and sits down on the back steps, Rick and Marshall join him on the steps. He tosses a snickers bar to Rick and Marshall. "Good looking out I was starving," Rick says as he tears open the wrapper and proceeds to eat. Tamir glances over the steps and sees everyone eating their snickers. "What? You ain't got one for me? I can't believe you're feeling some type of way, whatever man". Tim takes a few bites and with a mouthful begins speaking very matter of factly while cutting his eye at Tamir. "Like I was saying, I'm giving ya'll an opportunity to make money, as you can see, I'm already good I'm just trying to share the wealth." Marshall cutting Tim off mid-sentence "I think it's a great idea". Rick interjects "my thing is, how many cars are we gonna have to wash per day to make that much loot? Tim shakes his head "That's why I said there's a difference from just washing a car and detailing. Every car that is sold on my dad's lot I do, then I always leave my card in the ashtray to get that repeat business if I can". Just then, the ice cream truck theme song could be heard loud and clear like clockwork it was exactly 11 Am. Tim hops off the back porch, rushes up the driveway to the front of the house to see exactly where the truck is so he could get to it first. The truck as luck would have it or by coincidence was parked right in front of his house. He approaches the side of the open window "Ramirez, what it is?" Ramirez automatically went into the freezer to pull out 4 strawberry éclairs as he had become accustomed to doing, bringing them back to the window. "This is what it is my man, 4 éclairs' like always," he said with a smile. "I should've told you, I'm switching things up a bit today, just give me one," Tim said while counting out two singles from his handful of cash. "Only one? I guess your boys must not be over here today huh? He remarked. "Nope, they're here, just in the back, I think they need to know what it is to work like you and me!" He said as he was about to put the rest of the money back in his pocket, but then unfolded 3 more singles and gave them to Ramirez. "Ah, I understand that bro, what's this for? The éclair is only $1 you know" all the while putting the money in his pocket. Tim glances over to the right at the other kids on their way to the ice cream truck. "Let's just say I feel like being generous to people who will appreciate it, enjoy your day man," Tim spoke and thought like he was in his 30's trapped in a 14-year-old body. From birth, it seems he always been very mature and apparently endowed with an excellent work ethic. But those qualities were considered to be both good and bad traits depending on who you asked. He frequently dealt quite harshly with his friends, but his intentions were always good, he just wasn't the one for playing games. He walks back into the backyard where there is a game of rough house going on. He opens his ice cream takes a seat on the gray cement steps and yells "Yo, what's it gonna be? Are ya'll in or out? As he continues eating his ice cream. Tamir dribbles the ball over to the steps, the others come as well. They say with a unified voice "let's do it". Tim leans forward from the relaxed position he was in "Great! So here's the deal, later on we head down to my dad's dealership and fill these buckets up with dollars, feel me? All right let's get out of here".

A WALK IN THE PARK

Tim hops onto his white BMX bike with red trim and red spokes that was leaning against the side of the house. The rest of the guys followed on foot toward Clark Lake Park a short distance from Tim's house. Once upon a time Clark Lake Park was the epicenter of this once highly acclaimed part of the city. It was 5 acres of beautiful lush landscaped trees, shrubs, exotic flowers of various assortment. Boasting two gigantic gazebos this easily became the most sought after place to have an outside wedding, birthday party, you name it, and this was the place. Plenty of walking trails, it even had a manmade waterfall that resembled Niagara Falls. Albeit a modest version, of course, but you could tell there was serious thought and consideration that went into the planning of this park. There was a beautiful Olympic size in ground pool and arguably the clearest lake you could find in any city in America. Moreover, this was also home to the Clarksville Love Fest, which was a free 3-day celebration the city would host to say thanks to the city residents. They would have all types of entertainment, carnival rides, musicians, artist, contest, prizes coupled with a wide variety of food to enjoy. The celebration became so popular that people from other cities started coming, with this in mind they began making you show your driver's license to gain entry. By and large this became an event everyone looked forward to all year round. Furthermore, in the winter they would bring in and give away Christmas trees for the holiday to those who were less fortunate. They would have coat drives, toy giveaways in addition to a soup kitchen that was open the entire month of December! Fast forwarding to the present, the city has struggled financially for last 15 years. Consequently, with budget cuts being made left and right the celebration landed on the non-essential expenditure list. City council said the upkeep of the park was continually going over the budget year after year. Sorrowfully enough after the initial outrage from the residents, people just got over it discontinuing the fight to maintain the funding of the park. Under those circumstances, C.L.P, as it has been so affectionately dubbed by the young people, is now no more than a rest haven for a lot of negative activity especially at night. The park now hosts 4 net-less basketball rims on a massively damaged court. In conjunction with a worn out, weather-beaten faded green turf that aspiring tennis players could practice on if they didn't mind facing imminent injury. In the same way that once beautifully landscaped lake to walk around is now infested with litter, debris and God knows what else. The pool has been out of use for years not to mention the manmade falls have stopped flowing to conserve the water. As a result of all this the park is now mostly occupied by teenagers who want to show off their cars, as well as their car systems. But on a positive note it was somewhere else to hang out at instead of your house which is why Tim liked going there. Stacy's house is on the way to the park so naturally Tim puts his kickstand down on his bike every time he passes by to see if she wants to tag along. This day he goes up to the front steps of Stacy's house which you could never mistake because the house has a huge white and pink awning hovering over the doorstep. Her older sister Monique opens the main door, but not the screen door "What you want?" Tim replies with a look of disgust because of her obnoxious attitude toward him "What do I want? I think we both know why I'm here. Can you just tell her I'm here". Stacy overheard the conversation, seated on the couch in the living room and comes to the door. "Hey, what's up Tim?" She says, pushing the screen door open looking squarely into his hazel colored eyes. "I'm good, I just wanted to see if you wanted to come with us to C.L.P?" he asked with a flirtatious smile. "Clark Lake Park this early? What's going on?" looking at Tim. "We'll, I need to have a little meeting with the fellas first, then I want to spend some time with you. You know, walk around, talk, and hold hands. Is that cool with you?" Tim says, looking behind to make sure the fellas are not within earshot to hear what he was saying. They boys were playing in the front of the driveway throwing the football Tamir brought. "Ok, sound cool, let me get my shoes on," Stacy said then closed the screen door and went back inside. Monique comes to the door, sees Tim still standing there and slams the white front door shut. Minutes later Stacy reopens the door and comes out wearing purple shorts and a white top with some very fashionable purple Nikes. Stacy was undeniably breathtaking, it seemed no matter what she put on Tim was pleased. She was not only beautiful on the outside but beautiful on the inside as well. Stacy and her family moved up from South Carolina at the beginning of the school year. She was genuinely sweet and ladylike at all times. She most likely acquired that mindset from her mother who competed in numerous beauty pageants in South Carolina. Stacy revealed this truth to Tim because he would always make mention of how different she was compared to other girls. She would always respond "I get it from my momma" followed by a smile that would light up any room. This was the first time Tim really started to take notice of the opposite sex without being afraid to express his feelings. His dad taught him early on about the importance of treating women with respect along with being sincere. Tim's approach was different than most of the guys in his neighborhood, even his crew. He would not waste words on girls he was not legitimately interested in, he was not easily pressured into proving his was "the man". His Aunt Betty always referred to him as an old soul which must have been true because his maturity level always outweighed his number age. At 14, he wasn't looking to be too serious, although he enjoyed hanging out with Stacy a great deal. All of a sudden, Stacy jumps off the four steps right in front of Tim. "Here I am! You weren't ready for that, were you?" she says beaming. "Uh, no I wasn't" looking amazed at her leaping ability. "Yeah, I'm pretty athletic in case you didn't know. I had to test out my new sneaks, gotta make sure they have that bounce. I want to play basketball next semester, I figure you can help me work on my game" she says all excited. "I like that idea, that way I get to see you every day when I'm done work." They both start walking down the front pathway to the sidewalk joining the guys who are still playing football. "Hey, wassup Stacy?" Tamir says as he grabs and holds the football that Marshall threw to him. "Sup ya'll," she says with a wave of the hand addressing all of them at once. Tim' hops back on his bike and they continue to the park, which is about a mile and a half from her house. "Oh, before I forget, I'm sorry about Monique slamming the door in your face like that, I don't know why she acts like that with you." Tim stops his bike, signals to Tamir to toss the football to him, after catching it he's now riding with one hand on the handlebar with the other cradling the football under his arm. "It's all right, I could tell she never really liked me. Don't know why though, it's not like I did anything to her". "She's just weird like that I guess, imagine having to live her, she can be a bit much to deal with at times," Stacy says rolling her eyes. "But as I think about it, when we first got here she thought you were cool when I first told her about you. Hmm, oh well" she said as she was contemplating what changed her opinion of Tim. They all continue walking through the neighborhood, observing the varying degrees of care given to each home on the long street. By looking at the neighborhood's tree-lined streets, white light poles in the middle of each home's front lawn. It wasn't hard to imagine that once upon a time this neighborhood was a beautiful place to live and raise a family. For whatever the reason there were a number of homes that the owners refused to do any maintenance to at all. Clearly, something had changed because while there was still a handful of well-kept properties there were far too many abandoned homes. As a result of this, the vacant homes became dwellings for squatters with the majority becoming drug houses. You could not help but to wonder, was it that the residents could not afford the upkeep or that they just stopped caring altogether? But one thing was clear Clarksville was not what it used to be. The gang finally makes their way to Clark Lake Park after crossing the intersection of Grand Ave & Central St. They go over to the basketball courts bypassing the swings and the monkey bars. The grass was overgrown in most areas of the park especially near the courts which were now unoccupied be as it was too early for the "ballers" to come out.

SECOND GO ROUND

"Ok, let's get a game of rough house going," Tamir says as he dribbles the ball out onto the chipped up concrete court to make a layup. "Hold up, I called you over to let ya'll know how business is gonna work. Afterward, we can hoop it up for a little" Tim said as he casually strolled over to the gray metal bleachers to take a seat. "Ya'll come on over here" he shouts, then leans over to Stacy, who is seated alongside him. "Hey, why don't you go shoot around for a little bit while I handle business real quick, Is that cool?" He strips the ball out of Tamir's hands who had dribbled up next to him and passes it to Stacy. "Yeah, that's cool just don't keep me over here too long, "she says with the ball in hand as she starts dribbling up the court towards the basket. "Remember it's all about form, the flick of the wrist," Tim says." Stacy makes a layup and yells back "Yeah, uh, okay that's great advice" in a sarcastic, playful voice. Tim laughs, then turns his attention to his friends who are all now seated on the bleachers "Okay fellas I just want to cover a few things before we go down to the dealership". All of a sudden loud music is heard blasting from a late 80's model black Honda Accord, that's fast approaching the parking area near the basketball court. "Hey, yall hold up," Tim says getting up from the bleachers Rick, Marshall, and Tamir follow suit. Somehow he sensed there was trouble brewing as he carefully watches the car come to an abrupt stop slightly hitting the curb. The music was still blaring, without delay out steps Darius on the passenger side, throwing both arms in the air, then slams the door shut. However, in the distance a white Ford Taurus is slowly approaching the parking lot area as well. "So what's up now punk? Ain't no security out here!" Darius yells from the car as he walks around the car to the trunk which is now open. "Oh boy, here we go again!" Rick says while pounding his fist against each other. Marshall and Tamir start cracking their knuckles in preparation for the ensuing battle that's about to take place. Stacy, who was down at the other end of the court, hears the shouting and heads back over to the bleachers where Tim and the guys are standing. Tim is staring straight ahead in Darius's direction Stacy positions herself directly in his view. "Hey, listen it's so not worth fighting I'm not the least bit interested in him and never will be, let's just go." Tim looks down into her lovely green eyes "Stacy, somethings are worth fighting for" he moves her gently to the side heading toward the car. He realized that sounded like a cool line that she would always remember if he subsequently got beat to death. He was by no means ready to face Darius at least this soon. The main question going through his mind was how did he know he would be at C.L.P? "Let's do this! You want more than a busted lip this time I see" he yells while moving closer. Then four other guys about the same height and weight of Darius, step out the Accord, one with a bat in hand. Meanwhile, the Taurus had pulled up and parked. Tim immediately started to rethink his last statement loudly in his mind. "Man, this guy is way too upset about getting a busted lip sheesh! God, if you can hear me, I could certainly use your help right now" he prayed inwardly. At this moment in time, there was only 500 feet between the two opposing forces. Tim's feet were leading him almost involuntarily yet he did not want to look like a punk by stopping the forward movement. Nonetheless he quickly turns his head to the left, then the right making sure his crew were with him. They were, Darius and his boys are forging ahead looking like a swat team dressed in all black from head to toe. In like manner, Tim and his crew advance forward until they are but inches from being face to face. Then the white door of the Taurus opens and a boisterous voice yells. "Hey, what are you boys doing over there" it was Pastor Ron, who works as a corrections officer by day, dressed in full uniform. He had just left his house going toward the direction of the park when he felt compelled to follow the black Accord. Without regard to his own safety, walks fearlessly right in the middle of the standoff, towering over them all. He was a professionally trained in Krav Maga an Israeli self-defense, which incorporates several other forms of martial arts all in one. Conversely, it also helped that he stood 6'8 and weighed 275lbs of sheer muscle. "Is there a problem here Tim? What ya'll doing here? I know you have somewhere better to be right now?" Pastor Ron said firmly with his deep booming voice. "Surely, there is a God," Tim said to himself. Darius, visibly upset, shaking his head, pacing back and forth in the middle of the basketball court. "Naw man, he's right where he needs to be to get his teeth knocked down his throat!" he says sharply to Pastor Ron. Pastor Ron squints his eyes, zeroing in on Darius's face. "Hey, wait, aren't you Darius Bartholomew Jones?" he asked as he gets directly in his face. Rick, Marshall, and Tamir burst into laughter. "Bartholomew?" Tamir says, "What kind of a name is that?" Darius is now heated like a tea kettle ready to whistle "Yo, who are you? And why are you trying to play me man" looking mad enough to bite Pastor Ron's head off if it were possible. Pastor Ron moves so close to Darius's face, he could probably detect every piece of food he had eaten for lunch. "I'm somebody that knows your momma, where you live and what goes on in that house. I also know you're that your brother Marcus is locked up in my jail. So, let's just assume I know more about you than you would like me to know. And while I'm making assumptions, I suppose you guys came to play basketball along with a little baseball it appears, based on that bat! Oh, and wait, my last assumption is that if you know what's best for you, you better get out of here now!" Darius is furious but steps back slowly with so much anger in his eyes that if looks could kill, both Tim and Pastor Ron would be dead. All things considered, the consequences of challenging Pastor Ron to a duel would not be in his best interest, as he turns to his friends. "Y'all, let's go! He looks at Tim "It still ain't over church boy, next time, you gonna need Jesus himself to save you, not your Pastor!" Pastor Ron still standing in the middle of the circle which he has now broken up says "You still here? And, um, Batman aka Jerome Brooks, (the holder of the baseball bat) your license is suspended good luck getting home. I don't want to see you guys on this side of town anymore". The guys disperse as fast as possible Jerome looks at Darius "Man, I better not get pulled over coming out here to beat this dude down, that's all I'm sayin'. You know I'm riding dirty, got me coming over here for your little stupid beef with this dude." In a matter of fact way implying that Darius would have to deal with another fight on his hands but this fight would involve Jerome.

SAVING GRACE

Straightaway, Darius and his crew drove off so fast they left burnt rubber marks in the in the pavement. As a result, Tim and his friends were standing in the middle of the basketball court with Pastor Ron. "Hey, why don't you guys split as well? It's no need to stay up here today. Stacy, tell your dad, I'll stop by tomorrow with the truck so we can go get that washing machine he's been asking about. By the way do you need a ride?" He says as the crew begins to walk back the same path in which they came. Pastor Ron extends his massive arm grabbing Tim by the shoulder pulling him into what looked like a one arm bear hug. Without hesitation, Tamir quickly answers Pastor Ron's question directed toward Stacy just when she was about to speak. "Nah, she's cool, I mean, I'll make sure she gets back safely sir." Pastor Ron looks at Tamir confused as to why he's answering for Stacy but nonetheless skeptically responds "Is that okay with you? I need to have a little talk with Mr. Tim here". "Yeah, I'll be fine Pastor but thanks though, I'll tell my dad about the washing machine," she said. At that point Pastor Ron smiles at her then begins walking to his car signaling for Tim to follow him over "Hop in son" he said. Tim is apprehensive at first, but reluctantly walks toward the car. He would much rather walk back with his friends, especially Stacy. All of a sudden Tim stops in his tracks and yells."I can't ride back with you, I almost forgot I rode my bike over here" he said hoping the excuse would provide him a way out of the ride home. "Oh no worries, that bike will fit perfectly in the back seat, it's only a little BMX, not a big ol 10 speed!" Pastor Ron says sensing Tim was looking for an excuse to deny the ride. Realizing no reason will suffice Tim decides to stop making excuses and accept the ride back. Thinking to himself "How bad could it be?" He runs back to the court gets on his bike and rides back toward the car jumping off the small curb, then puts the bike in the back seat. With the bike barely squeezing inside he closes the back door then gets in the front seat and closes the door. Not wasting any time Pastor immediately starts a conversation "So, tell me, what are you into these days? I haven't seen you down at the church in about a year's time. What? Does my breath stink or something? Is that what's been keeping you away?" Tim almost lets out a laugh. For those who knew Pastor Ron on a personal level they know he has a great sense of humor and a big heart. Luckily for Tim he knew the real side of Pastor because on the outside looking in, the pastor could be seen as a tremendous threat to any opposition. Three years ago when Tim's parents' divorce was finalized and Loretta took off to Arizona with his sister, his dad started going to the Lux Lounge after getting off work. He would often use the excuse that he was working late Tim knew the car dealership was not open past midnight. During this time, Robinson met and jumped feet first into a serious relationship with Sunny, who began to occupy all of his free time. The reality was that he was trying to get his mind off of his divorce by continually staying on the go. Pastor Ron was a good friend of Stacy's dad Johnny they had grown up together in the neighborhood before he moved south. He would usually visit their house around 10 pm to have Bible study with Johnny, who is housebound due to an undisclosed illness. Often times leaving after midnight while driving down the block Pastor Ron would notice Tim on the front steps. He would be on the steps in his chair with the game light reflecting on his face. The truth is he would be out there playing handheld game system for hours. Being the kind of guy Pastor, Ron is after seeing this scene play out 3 times in a row he became curious and pulled in the driveway one night to introduce himself. He asked if his parents were home, without hesitation Tim lied. He feared he would get taken away to child protective services, considering he was a minor being left alone in the house. Pastor Ron seemed to always know when Tim is not being truthful but, he also knew how to get the answers he needed anyway. He invited Tim along with his parents out to service two blocks away on Florence Ave. He also let him know that even if his parents couldn't come the church doors were always open. It just so happens Robinson and Sunny went away on a three-week cruise. His dad was so caught up in the planning and shopping for the cruise he neglected to stock the house with food. At first Tim was unconcerned but after virtually depleting his savings, he finally broke down and decided to go check to the church to get something to eat. As it turned out, he discovered he enjoyed the going to the church. From that point on Tim would start to come on a regular basis, initially because they would serve an incredible breakfast. The spread included Mama Rose's homemade blueberry biscuits topped with butter, which would just melt in your mouth. Secondly, because he found some great new friends to hang with. And lastly, it helped him get an understanding of how to pray and the purpose of it. "No, pastor, you breath doesn't stink. I've just been chilling, working and getting ready to start working even more" as he reclines his seat as far back as possible. "You know Tim, there's one thing I can always say about you man, you always had a good head on your shoulder. I can't front either, we miss you down at the church. You just up and disappeared on us". Pastor Ron is purposely driving slowly to maximize the rare opportunity to speak with him. Meanwhile, Tim, is reclined in the passenger seat looking out the window silently watching the houses go by. Then he notices Pastor Ron makes a left onto Florence, which leads down to the church. Nonetheless, he chose not to make mention of it. "Yeah man you know it's so funny running into you like that today. I was driving through the neighborhood and I saw those guys driving crazy fast, then I noticed one fool had the bat visible from the passenger side window. So me being me, I said I should probably follow these knuckle heads to see what was going on. And low and behold, I find you, I assume that the bat was for you, am I right?" Pastor Ron says as he looks over at Tim laying back still looking out the window. Tim responds in a very nonchalant manner "I guess it looked that way, but I was just coming to hang out with my friends. By the way, we passed my house". Pastor Ron continues down the road to his intended destination before speaking again. "Oh, yeah? I did, didn't I? My bad, I just thought it would be good for you to see some of your other friends. That's not a problem is it?" He said is a low tone. As cool as Tim wanted to appear he knew the truth was he was thankful to God the Pastor showed up when he did. Not for nothing seeing his other set of friends would be refreshing, as there was no pressure to live up to anyone's expectations.

FAMILY OF FRIENDS

"I, I, guess its cool, but I can't stay too long I have to get to the dealership. Like my dad says "if it don't make dollars, it don't make sense" Tim says. Pastor Ron laughed and shook his head as he turned into the parking lot of Clark Church of Christ. "Young man, I think those lines came from DJ Quick if I'm not mistaken" Tim gives him the side eye. "How's the family? I was never successful getting your dad down to the church. Have you heard from your mom? How is Sunny treating you? Hold on let me slow down, I'm hitting you with a lot of questions" he says as he drives in the practically empty parking lot. He drove past the non-working water fountain into the parking spot that read reserved for the pastor on the wooden sign. The pastor turns on the radio, Run DMC's down with the king is playing as he bobs his head singing along with the song. "Down with the king, uh, yeah, I like that tune right there. I wanna be down the king of kings. How bout you?" smiling looking over at Tim. However, Tim remains unamused as Pastor Ron is continuously trying to chip away at his hard exterior by making more jokes. "We'll, we're here! Says Pastor Ron as he reaches in the back seat getting his briefcase. "I need to drop off some paperwork before I go to work," he said as he takes the key out the ignition. After he gets out the car, he closes the door behind him. No sooner than he gets out Robbi, Pastor Ron's 14-year-old son runs full speed out the door full of excitement to him. "Hey dad, I just unlocked some new cheat codes on Mortal Kombat 3," Robbi said. Then immediately paused for a moment to make sure who he thought he saw next to him was correct. "Tim? Hey man, where have you been? I called only like 100 times man!" he said with his eyes bulging. Tim is allowing his eyes to roam to the left to try to think of a good excuse to give Robbi. He knows some type of explanation is needed for his untimely disappearance, feeling somewhat embarrassed after scanning his brain for an acceptable answer Tim replies. "It's good seeing you too, I've just been busy with school and work, you know how it goes." Pastor Ron gives Robbi a high five then walks toward the bright red double doors that lead to the church. "We'll I'm going to go grab some paperwork, ya'll can either come in or stay outside, I'll be right back. Pastor Ron goes in, the door closes behind him. Robbi and Tim are left outside, Tim begins to lift himself up and down on the curb giving his calf muscles a workout. Much like Tim, Robbi was certainly wise beyond his years and had a gift for his father. It was almost like a 6th sense which allowed him to be able to determine what was going on with someone without asking. Robbi wore thick red glasses that were always a bit too snug over his nose, he was a major wrestling fan, so he stayed in a printed Tee shirt of his favorite wrestlers. "We'll, let me just get to the point Tim, I think I speak for all of the youth here at the church in saying you let us down when you just rolled out on us! I mean we always had a good time together and it seems your other friends became more important than us" Tim looks speechless as he's listening intently to the words coming out of Robbi's mouth. "I mean I understand everyone has other friends and things to do. But we felt like your brothers and sisters, we accepted you as you are, you didn't have to buy us anything or put on an act for us. By the way how did you link up my dad again? Tim stops his training his calves bringing his feet on solid ground. "Wow, you have certainly grown up in a year's time young boy," He says in a sarcastic voice "We'll Robbi as if I have to explain myself to you. You pretty much said everything that was going on. The thing is ya'll are too uptight and stiff for me to hang around. "Tim pauses goes in the back seat grabs his bike out and takes a short lap around the lot and returns back to Robbi, who is standing anticipating an explanation of that last remark. Tim rides directly toward Robbi, who does not flinch as he stops the bike inches in front of him. "I see you got heart now, huh? You didn't flinch!" he says with a smug look on his face. Robbi places his hands on the handlebars, looks directly into Tims eyes "For God has not given me the spirit of fear, but of power, love, and a sound mind". Tim sucks his teeth and pushes Robbi's hands away. "See, that's exactly what I'm talking about. When I was around here that type of stuff was okay. But as I get older I want to do things that ya'll don't think about and honestly, I don't want to hear ya'll input on". Robbi focuses his eyes on the beautiful green trees as he takes a seat on the curb contemplating the right response. "Look, we're gonna love you either way, like I said we family and were not gonna just throw you away because you feel a need to explore what you call life. I guess I act the way I act because all my life, I've heard the issues of almost every church member who came to the house to get prayer and counseling from my dad. The main thing I learned is that for everyone who went out to so call live and explore all the crazy things this life has to offer. They only returned back to their knees asking God to help them in some kinda way. I guess I prefer to learn from others" he says wiping off the back of his pants off rising to his feet. "Preach on Preacher, amen!" Tim says while stomping his feet down on the pavement, clapping his hands. Acting out the motions of a stereotypical Baptist preacher in an attempt to mock him. "We'll, it's no wonder what you're gonna do when you grow up." Just then, Pastor Ron comes rushing out the door toward the car, gives Robbi another high five "Alright young man, your mom will be back here up to get you. Make sure you lock all the doors and cut the lights off, I'm gone. Tim, you ready to roll?" Tim nods takes another quick lap around the parking lot. He rides back up to the car door puts the bike back inside closes the door, and opens the front passenger door but does not get in right away. He puts his left arm around the door looks at Robbi as he walks up to the car a walks up to the car and says. "Good seeing you man, hopefully not for the last time." Tim looks down at Robbi's extended hand and shakes it firmly "We'll see". Pastor Ron is now in the car and is backing out of the parking spot "So, did you guys have a chance to catch up? Tim decides to finally pull the seat up "Yeah we did". Pastor Ron is smiling as he cuts on the air conditioner that is barely blowing cold air. "That's good, that's good. I'm not gonna front, I certainly miss you hanging around with the rest of the young folk. You know I ain't never been one to get in the people business, okay well maybe a little, but I'm a little concerned about you. These streets are rough and we both know there is plenty of trouble to get into in Clarksville". "Pastor listen, that situation today was crazy" deciding to open up to him. "I just have a lot going on in my world right now man, you don't understand." Nearly at Tim's street "Yeah, you may be right, I don't understand your particular situation, but I'm sure I've seen something like it before" Pastor Ron says still smiling. "Really? Well, have you ever jammed your evil step mom's fingers in a drawer before?" Tim says in a very condescending voice. Pastor Ron slams his foot on the brake pedal "What? You slammed her fingers in the drawer?" He said looking at Tim. "Yeah, but not on purpose, so of course I gotta explain that to my dad when I get back" turning his head out toward the window. Pastor continues driving and now pulls into Tim's driveway puts the car in park but keeps the engine running. "Yeah, you're right that's gonna be an interesting conversation, but all you can do is tell the truth and I'm sure all will be fine. I'm gonna get out of here now, but you know I'm always available if you want to talk about anything." Tim looks at Pastor Ron nods his head and gets out the car then proceeds to get his bike out the back seat. Once the bike is out, he leans it on the kickstand and opens the front door. "Thanks again Pastor." "Anytime young man, tell your dad I said hi, will ya?" as he puts the car in the reverse gear and speeds off down the street. Meanwhile Rick, Tamir, Marshall, and Stacy are walking back home. "This is getting ridiculous, so what, every time we see this fool Darius it's gonna be a problem? Marshall says as he tosses the football up in the air. Tamir runs out 30 feet in front of Marshall then says "Yo, throw it to me!"

he does and they pass the ball back and forth along as they continue talking. Rick walking next to Stacy as they advance down the street responds "I certainly hope not, this is getting a be a big problem". "Darius is the biggest loser ever! He came all the way across town to start trouble" says Tamir as he catches the football nearly preventing a fall as his foot almost landed in the unseen ditch on the lawn he just ran into. "Come to think of it, how did he know Tim would be up there? Rick says with a puzzled look on his face as the near Grand Ave. "That really is a good question, like what are the chances of him just magically appearing at the park minutes after we get there." Soon they approach Stacy's house where they find Monique sitting on the front steps looking surprised as they approached the house. "Why ya"ll back so soon?" she exclaimed. "And where is your boy Tim? While looking at Stacy, who waves bye to the fellas and approaches the front steps and responds. "What's it to you Monique? I already know you don't like him. The question is why? But on second thought, I don't even care to hear why" Stacy annoyed with her sister's attitude, especially with everything that took place at the park. "Move out the way, you're blocking the steps!" She bumps Monique's leg on purpose as she heads to open the screen door. Monique rolls her eyes and looks at Stacy as if she had a third eye and says "Little girl, you better watch yourself before you get beat down like you're little boyfriend." Stacy goes in the house and speaking from the door "Whatever" as she goes past the kitchen down the hall to her bedroom, she thinks did she just hear what she thought she heard. "What does she mean beat down like my boyfriend? How in the world could she know about that?" The phone rings Monique comes in the house to grab the phone and goes back out onto the porch. Stacy noticed the light on the phone that indicated it was in use was red and crept out her room back to the front door to hear who she was talking to. She stood in the back of the door listening hard "Hey, what happened? I told you they were going up there" Monique said in a whispering voice. Stacy heard the rest of the conversation and went back to her room to think about what to do with what she just heard.

DADDY'S DILEMMA

Robinson is sitting down in a worn out green fabric chair behind his warped wooden oak desk, inside his small dark wood paneled office. He picks up a few pieces of papers that are scattered all over the desk. Most have overdue notices stamped in red on them. After scanning several papers, he eyes are fixated on one sheet that says eviction, must evacuate premises immediately. Consequently, Robinson is showing signs of major distress, allows his forehead to hit the stack of papers on his desk full force hoping to be knocked unconscious. The attempt was unsuccessful, but it did leave him with a big bruise on his forehead. "How am I going to explain this to everyone?" he says to himself. He gets up from the desk paces back and forth then glances out the window. Now paralyzed in his tracks as he notices several flatbeds have arrived to pick up the few vehicles that remain. He began visualizing his whole life flashing before his face as people do before death. He was secretly dealing with alcoholism after the divorce from his wife years earlier. To add to his woes, Sunny is a big gambler, their dates often began and ended in the casino. Sunny liked the attention of the heavy rollers, so to keep her around he kept up that facade to appease her. As a result, this lifestyle quickly brought about the financial trouble, which ultimately lead to the demise of his business. One night Sunny was playing blackjack, a simple game. Each numbered card along with face card has a value to it, to win you need to come as close as you can to getting 21 without going over that number. We'll this night Sunny got way in over her head, resulting in her losing 10 thousand dollars that Robinson had saved. She begged Robinson to take out a loan at the casino so she could attempt to win back the money she had lost. He reluctantly did as she asked, but was not able to recoup the money and lost another 10 thousand dollars. They both leave the table headed toward the exit, when Sunny who is totally intoxicated at this point pushes Robinsons shoulder "Hey, I know we're not gonna leave here as losers? You can make 10 thousand anytime from selling cars right? Mr. big shot? I'm telling you I can win tonight, I feel it" as she staggers toward the ladies room. Foolishly Robinson agrees and gets a wire transfer for 10 thousand dollars forwarded to his account. They returned to the table and Sunny hit! She went on a lucky streak, winning 7 thousand dollars, it was at this point she decided to press her luck looking to win big. She bets all the money she had on the next turn and loses it all. After losing, Robinson immediately makes a b line for the door, without looking back once for Sunny. He was extremely upset, weeping with tears streaming down his face. Sunny eventually caught up with him at the car and at that point she made a verbal agreement with him as they rode back. They both agreed it was necessary she make monthly payments to reduce the debt. Unfortunately for Robinson, she had no intention of repaying the money, but she felt it was best to keep the peace until she found another plan. Sunny made one payment on the account then afterwards blamed Robinson for letting her gamble. Robinson doesn't want to disappoint his new found love so after being quilted, started making payments on the loans. But he was falling under fast as the profits from his auto business were drying up. Jobs were becoming scarce in Clarksville so with a lot of the factories closing up so people began to move out of town to find work. With fewer people buying cars meant the cost of doing business was becoming impossible. All this was happening just a year and a half into the relationship causing issues Tim never knew about. Robinson watches from the open door as the workers load the last vehicle on the back of the flatbed almost in tears. The marshal knocks on the partly open door and says "It's time" in a solemn voice. Robinson grabs his brown leather jacket off the back of the chair and grabs his keys off his desk. Pauses taking a big breath of air as he looks around at the now bare office walls. He walks out and closes the door behind.

ONE HAPPY FAMILY

Robinson stops by the corner store to purchase a for sale sign which he plans to put on his Mercedes. He figures if he can sell the car it will keep them afloat financially for about 3 months. Riding slowly through the neighborhood, he approaches the house prepared to tell everyone the news with no hesitation. However, as he pulls in, Sunny sticks her head out the door waving him inside as if the house is on fire. She's overly excited to tell him everything that took place earlier. He pulls into the backyard cuts the car off, takes a few deep breaths and a swig of brandy from his flask, and then exits the vehicle. He pulls the cap off the marker and begins to write his number on the sign, which he placed on top of the hood. Much to his dismay, he's interrupted by Sunny coming out the house in a rage, waving her now bandage fingers supported by a splint at him. "Look at this! You see this? She exclaimed with anger throwing her broken fingers in his face. "THIS, is what your son has done to me!" Robinson stops writing entirely and focuses his attention on Sunny. She puts her fingers virtually in his eyes. "Your son did this to me! He's out of control and you better do something about it". Robinson gently grabs her hand to remove it from his face "How in the world did this happen? I'm sure it was a mistake whatever it was, he wouldn't intentionally do anything to hurt you". She's enraged by his seemingly immediate defense of Tim. She gives him a look that would kill the strongest opponent in the world if it were possible, then storms off toward the house. Robinson runs from behind to catch up with her, he grabs her arms. "Hey, hey, slow down. I'm just saying there has to be a real explanation behind all this". Sunny stops and looks back at him with disgust "This is what I'm talking about, without even knowing the details you take his side. This madness must and will stop I don't feel safe with him here anymore" She breaks his grasp and goes into the house. Robinson watches her go in the house and just looks up at the sky gazing at the sun which is now beginning to set. "God, I really don't need this right now, I just wanted to say what I had to say and got to bed." He turns back to go get the for sale sign he left on the top of the hood then goes to the back door. Mentally exhausted, he proceeds up the steps to face the impending drama. As he enters the house, he sees Sunny sitting at the kitchen table, leaning back in the chair with arms folded impatiently waiting. "So?" she says. "Baby, listen I have something that I need to share with both of you that's important. But I guess that will have to wait until later. Calmly, tell me what happened?" He puts the for sale sign on the counter goes to the refrigerator grabs a bottled water and sits down at the table with Sunny. "It's simple, your son is disrespectful and violent. All I did was come in his room and he slammed my fingers in the drawer!" No sooner than she could get the words out of her mouth Tim walks into the kitchen, calmly leans on the wall and says "Dad, that's a lie. You have such bad taste in women! I can't believe you allow this woman to make a fool out of you" Sunny jumps up from the table "Do you hear this disrespect? This is what I'm talking about!" Tim really didn't mean to utter those words, but they just came out. "Tim, watch yourself," he said in a serious tone. "You know what dad, this needed to be said a long time ago I typically hold it in, but I'm not any longer. For starters, she came into my room without knocking, which is wrong! Comes over in my personal space while I'm in my drawer getting my things, talking crazy. Apparently her fingers got caught when I slammed the drawer case closed. However, looking back at it I'm glad it happened." Sunny still standing with her back against kitchen counter "He saw my fingers Robinson, you just heard him say he's happy it happened what more do you need? He's nothing but trouble" Robinson sat up in his chair "Sunny, sit down, everybody just calm down". "Calm down? She says, "I'm the one with the broken fingers and you're telling me to calm down?" Tim pushes himself off the wall looking to escape outside. "Look, I'm done with this," he says. Robinson jumps up in front of him as he passed by the table, Tim and Robinson are almost neck to neck in height even though time is 14. Robinson raises his voice. "Hey! Where are you going? And what's with this attitude?" Tim looks directly into his father's eyes "She don't want me here that's obvious, so I'm leaving". A momentary stare down ensues between the two and neither one is looking to back down. But after a fierce look from Robinson, Tim finally backs down. He grabs his cap off the kitchen counter, heads down the steps leading to the back door of the house. "Tim, wait! Robinson yelled. "I'm not done talking to you boy! Get back here right this second" At the same time Tamir, Marshall and Stacy have arrived at the back door. They overheard all the drama from the open kitchen window. Tamir looks at Stacy and says "Yo, Stacy I think you should knock on the door. I'm not trying to get cussed out" laughing in a playful way. Stacy gives Tamir a wrinkled face look "Um, so you rather I get cussed out?" as she turns to walk away. Tamir runs after her, she stops "I'm pretty sure if you go to the door, they will calm down." He says putting his arm around her shoulder gently turning her around leading her back to the door. "We'll, you might be right. But I'm running if I see some pots and pans being thrown." Stacy chuckles walking toward the door but before she can knock on the door, she sees Tim through the screen door in a yet another stare down with Robinson. Robinson had jumped up to chase after Tim because he did not stop when he told him to. Sunny meanwhile with a wicked grin on her face walks closer to the back door to further inflame the situation "Yeah, you can't let him disrespect you like that. What you gonna do?" She says with an attitude with her arms crossed. In all the years, Tim and Robinson have lived together they have never come face to face in a confrontational way until today. There was so much tension in the air you could cut it with a knife. Robinson feeling the pressure decides to stand his ground, especially in light of the fact that his actions or inaction would now shape the way Sunny viewed him once and for all. Sunny was just looking to destroy their bond and continue to use Robinson. Robinson grabs Tim up by the collar, "Boy, don't you walk away from me when I'm talking!" Tim angrily tries to loosen himself out of the hold to no avail. All the while Tamir and Stacy are watching the scene play out through the door. Stacy decides to go ahead and knock on the door in hopes of distracting the two. Her plan works, Robinson glanced at Stacy then loosens his grip at which point Tim is freed. He pushes the door open with all his might, breaking the hinge, nearly missing Stacy. It's now dark outside, Tim walks hastily past Tamir and Stacy, brushing past Marshall who chose to avoid listening to the drama he stayed at the bottom of the driveway. Tim makes his way up the pitch black street which is illuminated by a single street light directly in front of Tim's house. "Hey, where you going bro?" Marshall says as he jogs to catch up with him. Tamir and Stacy follow behind they each look at each other with an uncertainty as to when or if they should speak. By this time Tim is marching down the street toward the park, everyone eventually catches up with him. Tamir shrugs his shoulders and says to Stacy "I guess I'll be the one to break the silence.""Yo man, I thought you were gonna knock your dad out, I ain't never seen you that mad!" Tim stops in his tracks and goes up to Tamir and hits him square in the eye with a closed fist and knocks him to the ground. Tamir's eye swells up fast Marshall and Stacy gasp at the site of the damage. Marshall rushes to the ground hovering over Tamir to prevent Tim from doing any more damage. Looking up at Tim Marshall says "Yo, calm down dude, ya'll ain't supposed to be fighting like this!"Tamir is visibly shaken up but responds angrily "Man, I can't help that you and your family is crazy! What you hit me for? I'm gonna jack you up, you gonna get yours" Tim continues alone toward the park without uttering a sound. Marshall pulls Tamir back to his feet while Stacy shakes her head, "You say the dumbest things Tamir! What's wrong with you? Marshall cleaning off the dirt from his pants, checking for grass stains, Tamir begins to do the same. Stacy looks at Tamir with disgust shakes her head "You say and do the dumbest things, you deserve that black eye you got. What happened was no laughing matter at all fool!" As she turns walking the same direction as Tim. She pulls out a pink key chain flashlight, with a little canister of mace dangling from it pointing in Tim's direction. Tamir still a little dazed holding his eye walking toward the park with Marshall gets irate. "Man, forget him and forget all of y'all too! That's why I'ma get Darius to come to tear him to pieces, he got lucky the first time but not no more" Marshall "Whoa, wait, what? Did you have something to do with that? I hope I'm not hearing what I'm hearing" Marshall comes to a complete standstill awaiting a response. Tamir continues feverishly brushing his pants off with a grimace on his face. "Look, man, I don't care what you heard or what you tell him. Matter fact go ahead and tell em what you want. He ain't gonna be punkin' me no more. Stacy should be with me anyway". Marshall's face becomes visible as the house light comes on in front of a neighbor's house. "You mean to tell me that you would set up your friend over a girl that doesn't even like you? You're a real sucka!" Marshall says, shaking his head. Just then the front door opens and Robinson sticks his head out and sees the kids down the street and yells. "Eh, you boys seen where Tim went?" Tamir looks at Robinson and just walks off in the dark. Marshall comes up to the front steps where Robinson is peeking his head out the screen door in a white tank top. "Naw, sir, I ain't seen him in a few minutes, but I think he's headed up to CLP. Stacy might be on her way up there with him though" Robinson's face is showing signs of worry, "Oh ok, thanks, young man, be cool". Robinson closes the screen door back and Marshall says in a low solemn voice "you too". Inside the house, after Robinson closes the door, he slams his back against the door with his head looking up. "Lord, what should I do?" Glancing over at the half empty bottle of wine sitting on the cluttered table with mail and circulars sprawled about. Then, as if a light bulb goes off in his head, he gets puts a smile on his face. Excited he proclaims "I'm gonna go get my son, he ain't staying out here alone in these streets". Sunny overhearing Robinson talking aloud to himself, comes to the door and stares at Robinson. "You go running after that evil son of yours and were through " She declared. Robinson's blissful smile quickly turned into a grimace as he looked at her as if she were transparent. "Well, that's a chance I'm going to take tonight Sunny. Come to think of it, what kind of person are you anyway? What has my son done to you outside of exist? For the longest time, I tried to just ignore the side remarks you would often make. But looking back, my son never gave me any real problems. On that note, you're welcome to leave whenever you feel like it, so don't wait up". He grabs his keys off the table, and his black jacket from off the arm of the chair and walks out the back door to get his car. Once inside the car after starting the ignition he pauses with both hands on the steering wheel then says a prayer. "Father, I know I don't call on you too often for anything, but I need you to help my relationship with my son. And, by the way, could you lead me right to him? Thanks". Feeling confident his prayers will be answered, he backs out the driveway and heads down the dark street being lit by his headlights.

SEARCH BUT DON'T FIND ME

Meanwhile, Stacy is approaching her house on the way to look for Tim and hears a male voice call out from a black car. She almost recognizes the voice but is not sure so she comes a little closer to the vehicle to see who it is. "Del, is that you?" she asked, thinking it was her older cousin. Just then both the passenger and the back door on the right side of the car opens. Two men jump out and grab her before she could let out a yell. It appeared that no one was home in Stacy's house because all the lights were out. This day, however, her father mustered up enough strength to sit in his favorite chair in front of the window. He was eagerly anticipating her return because it was getting late. After hearing the first car door slam, he moved the curtain open and saw Stacy being shoved into the back seat. He is still so weak, but attempted to get up, in his haste fell down hitting his head on the coffee table and was knocked unconscious. Now with both car doors closed and what they thought were no witnesses, the kidnappers drive off slow as to not draw the attention of the police who were just two blocks up. Simultaneously, Tim is at the park which is now closed, he's sitting on the stone edge of the old waterfall. There is a glimmer of light shining on him courtesy of the moon. He digs into his pockets and pulls out a few crumpled up dollars "Now what?" he thinks to himself. "I guess I should just roll out of here, I got money, and if I'm gone, so are my problems." He says while unfolding and counting the bills. In the distance, he sees lights from a car pull into the heavily wooded park near the basketball courts. The light shines a beam right on him, Tim hopes it's not his dad or worse the cops. He stuffs the money back into his pockets and takes off running toward Central Street. Robinson sees a figure moving and immediately gets out the car. With the lights left on, engine running he starts running through the basketball court almost falling due to the broken concrete. "Tim, Tim, is that you son? Stop! Tim, if that's you, Stop!" he screamed at the top of his lungs to no avail. The mystery person had immediately vanished out of sight. Tim heard the calls of his dad but decided to continue running to Central Street as luck would have it the 618 bus was pulling up so he got on. The 618 runs into the heart of the city and stops at the Clark Central Station. There you can catch a bus to virtually anywhere you wanted to go. On the bus ride over Tim's forehead is pressed against the hard plastic windows looking out on the streets watching people moving about. Some were homeless, some were going into Lucy's Bar N Grille, where patrons could get more than just beer and wine. It was also the hangout spot to some of the biggest drug dealers in CLP, as the bus nears the station Tim is in deep thought. Should he go away or not he thought to himself, not forever, but some time away would be refreshing he supposed. "Everybody off, this bus is no longer in service," says a portly female bus driver who looked worn out from driving all day. Tim gets up and moves slowly to the front of the bus as the driver is leaning over the driver seat, gathering her purse and taking the keys out the ignition. "Hey, young man, where you going by yourself this late? Ain't yo folks expectin you" she said in a southern drawl. Tim keeps silent and proceeds down the steps "HEY! You ain't hear me boy?" she yelled. He was startled, certainly not expecting her to raise her voice or even repeat her question. With anger written all over his face, he turns back looking up the steps and mumbles "I'm good" then quickly walks into the station. "That boy ain't doing nothin but running away, I see it all the time," the bus driver says to herself. With coat and purse on her arm, she comes down step by step slowly holding on to the rail. After making sure, the bus door was closed she reaches in her bag and grabs her walkie talkie. "Retha, listen, I think this little boy on my bus is runnin' away, he can't be no older than Jordan and he's only 14. Let the guards know so they can check him out". Retha responds via the walkie talkie "you always swear these kids be runnin' away, you crazy, I'll call it in." This was Tim's first time at the station as he had never traveled out of town via bus, so he's quickly reading the signs trying not to look like a tourist. He figures he will just hop on the first bus leaving, so he heads to the counter with a neon green display that read New Franklin. Just under it was a billboard showing a departure time in 2 minutes. At the ticket counter was an older white man with wrinkled pink skin, crooked glasses a dingy white shirt and yellow stained teeth. His was sipping his coffee slowly and clearly in no rush. "Can I help you?" he said. As Tim digs into his pockets for his money, he felt eyes on him so he looked over to his left. Low and behold there was a woman talking to security looking in his direction. He assumes the bus driver must have said something. He starts sweating and talking fast "Hey man, give me a ticket here's $20 I gotta catch this bus". "We'll everybody know it doesn't cost no $20 to go to New Franklin," he said in a slow southern accent. Tim is sensing they may be talking about him so he tenses up "hey man, how much is it? The bus bout to leave dude!" he says anxiously. He starts scanning the station with his eyes, primarily for exits and the gates. "Gate $7, it's only $10, he's ya change and your ticket," the guy at the counter says in what seemed like slow motion. No sooner than he hands him the ticket the security starts walking toward him. The male guard yells "Hey you, stay right there". Tim is not having it and takes off full speed down the corridor through the glass doors and hops onto the bus before the door closes. The guards almost make it to the bus as it's backing out of the garage. The bus driver was too busy looking out of his rear mirror on his left side to notice, off they go.

GRAND WELCOME

Out of breath, Tim lays back in the seat, relieved that he escaped the guards. With his head pressed against the back of the seat, he's thinking about his whole situation, wondering what he plans to do once he arrives. The bus moves rapidly down the street going under the underpass heading toward the New Franklin Parkway. He pulls out the crumpled dollars again to continue adding up his money, which added up to $82. Tim takes a deep breath, presses the button to bring his seat back to the upright position and stares out the window. He has a bewildered look on his face as he contemplates exactly how long he will be able to survive on such a small amount of cash. One thought was just to get to the station and hop back on the bus and go home. But, on the other hand, he wants his dad to get a chance to miss not having him around. New Franklin was only 30 minutes away, and a decision will soon have to be made as to what was going to take place next. The city of New Franklin has a population of about 8 million people. Not the type of place to hang out alone, not to mention having only $82 on you. In the midst of racking his brain for answers, the bus pulls into the station. The bus driver is given the green light to pull forward into his designated spot by a worker. The overhead lights come on, passengers began moving around, grabbing their luggage from the overhead compartments then rushing to the exit. Soon the bus is empty, and the male driver proceeds down the aisle to do a final check and sees Tim with his eyes closed in the chair. "Hey, son!" He shouts. "You got to get movin'." Tim awakens shaken up by the bus drivers thunderous voice, turns his heads to the right, focusing his eyes on the bus driver. "Huh, what?" He says, wiping the sleep from his eyes. "Were here, New Franklin?" the bus driver says as he turns his back heading to the front of the bus to exit. "Oh yeah, that's right, we are here Tim says assuredly not wanting to seem like it was his first time in the big city. Tim takes a final look out the window, then proceeds down the aisle to the steps of the bus. It's now 11:15 as his feet touches the ground. A broad mix of emotions is going on in his mind at the same time. The realization that he was in New Franklin was as exciting as it was scary. The bus terminal was a hub filled with what appeared to be hundreds, if not thousands of people moving at the speed of light throughout the busy terminal. Once inside the gates, he begins taking it all in as he walks through the station taking mental pictures of the various sights. It was like a huge mall, numerous stores, and vendors selling everything from Gold chains, watches, to little toys along with plenty of food options to choose. New Franklin is famous for many things and pizza is certainly one them, he goes into Brick Oven Kitchen to grab a slice. After waiting in line for at least 30 people to get their food. He finally gets his 2 slices and takes a seat near the window facing the busy street. Out the window, he looks in awe at the bright lights displaying advertisements on huge billboards posted onto massive buildings. Hundreds, if not thousands of people are walking by so fast it looked like they were running. He knew for sure he was certainly nowhere close to the place that he called home. One passerby a man who appeared to be in his late 20's flashily dressed, with a gold cap on his head, his body adorned with gold chains along with what appeared to be a Rolex watch. His fingers held gold rings filled with diamonds shining so bright you could see the sparkle in the mirror. For reasons unknown to Tim the man comes to a complete stop in front of the window and looks directly at him. Tim is holding up the gargantuan greasy pepperoni slice of pizza about to enter it into his mouth when he looks up and notices the man staring him directly in his face. Tim could not figure out if the man wanted to make trouble or just wanted to eat his pizza. After a roll of the eyes, Tim takes a bite of the pizza and savors every moment of it. Coincidentally, the man moves out of sight once he was spotted staring. People continue coming and going in front of the window as Tim enjoyed his people watching experience. With the pizza gone, he just sipped on his soda, a man approaches with an apron around his waist, extremely hairy arms exposed comes up to the table with a wet cloth in hand. "Excuse me, sir, are you done eating? I need the table space for customers to eat" he says with an undoubtedly strong Middle Eastern accent. The voice breaks his focus, he was in a slight daze taking in the new scene. All at once he looks up at the face of the man behind the voice. Then back to his drink, which he takes a sip of, then takes his attention back to the window. "Um, well I'm still finishing my drink," he says without taking a second glance at the man. The man puts the cloth down on the table with both hands extended and clears his throat. "Young man, I, I, cannot afford to tie up a seat while you just finish a drink. I'm going to have to ask you to leave". Tim in disbelief turns back to the man "I didn't know there was a time limit on eating around here!" he fires back at the man. Tim decides it's better to just avoid getting into a confrontation that could lead him into trouble. Slowly gets up leaving his paper plates along with napkin on the table squeezes his way through the crowd and heads out the door onto the busy sidewalk.

SEEN ME BEFORE SEE ME AGAIN

Shortly after exiting the door, Tim begins pondering where exactly he expects to sleep for the night. Without much thought, he decides to head east on the Chalfont Blvd the most popular strip in the whole city. Chalfont offered a vast array of attractions, casinos, hotels, and restaurants you name it, and it was there. Most of the upscale entertainment was located on the West side of the strip. With this in mind heading east, you would find a more than a subtle change in atmosphere. Needless to say, very few ventured down that end at night except the brave of heart. After walking about 2 miles on the strip, Tim staggers back when a man suddenly comes crashing through the front window of Slick City, a shabby looking dive bar. At that instant, another man who had to be at least 350 pounds comes out and starts punching the already bloodied man on the pavement in the face. Consequently, Tim speeds up his walk until he gets to the window seal of a store which had an extended ledge for him to sit down on. It is now 1 a.m. in the morning, his feet and legs were begging for a break from all his aimless walking. What was initially fun had now turned to grief as he is still wondering where he is going to sleep tonight. At this point, he's utterly discouraged so he puts his head down on his lap, pulling his hood over his head. Though it was summer the temperature drops considerably low at night, he was cold and sleepy. He slowly drifts off into a light sleep when all of a sudden a nudge on his left shoulder wakes him up. Tim swiftly lifts his head up from his lap, immediately on the defensive swipes at the hand that he saw was extended about to nudge him again. Tim looks up into the face of the man who he saw earlier outside the pizza shop. His eyes at that moment showed a combination of fear and uncertainty as to what should be his next move. Fight or take Flight was the question that needed to be answered quickly. He decides to make an attempt to fight so he stands up. But the man full of gold though only a few feet taller than him pushes him down back down, his back bangs against the glass. Tim makes another attempt to get back up fast as possible just then the man of gold unzipped his jacket, opens it wide enough for Tim to see the butt of his gold-plated pistol. "Look homie, I don't think you wanna do that, you better relax! Clearly you ain't from around here, get up let's walk." At this point, Tim has surrendered any plans he had to fight the man of gold once the gun was shown. The man lightly grips the collar of Tim's jacket, prompting him to get up. He reluctantly gets up from the concrete seat, giving the man a dirty look while straightening out his jacket. "Look man, I think you got me mixed up with somebody else. You need to let me just go about my business! I'm meeting family here any minute, they got bigger guns than you!" Tim exclaimed as he begins walking, being lead down the street by the unnamed man. They slowly approach the Shogun Casino parking garage. This stretch of the Boulevard is where Tourist usually turns around and go back up to the west end. This area was dubbed "D City" Gone are the expensive hotels, fancy restaurants, high-end shopping stores. This area is overwhelmed with drugs, drug dealers, street workers, low budget motels, one shoddy casino and plagued with high crime. For this reason, only those who are a part of this lifestyle dare venture into this area especially at night. The 13 story casino itself looks all but vacant, the windows are completely covered with outdated posters which are torn and tattered. Several light bulbs are missing from the old fashion sign protruding from the brick wall. There's trash blowing up and down the street thanks to the gusty winds reminiscent of the wild wild west. "Eh, go up this way" the man shoves Tim toward the garage entrance all the while looking all around for any potential eyes that may be watching. Tim starts sweating profusely all over his body. His forehead begins to drop beads of sweat, his hands were virtually dripping. He adjusts his sweat soaked collar, while taking a big gulp, trying to swallow down the fear that has taken a grip. The man watched him carefully as they both entered the garage. A number of thoughts started running around in his head from the good to the bad to the outrageous. How great it would be if he were in his room watching his TV, eating a strawberry éclair he imagined. Who would have thought so much enjoyment could come from something as simple as an ice cream? Then he thought, well, just how good would it actually be to be at home? After all, he was running away to escape the drama in his everyday life. He still has this ongoing dispute with Darius, which he figures is going to surface again. He still has to deal with Sunny manipulating his dad ruining their relationship. His mom has yet to call or return to see him. But all things considered nothing could compare to this current predicament. In his mind, the reality is that his life was now on the line and all for what he thought. He never missed his Dad, Stacy, and home so much in all his life before tonight. Just then he realizes he has to do something, his survival instinct kicks in once again. "If I'm going down, I'm going down with a fight" he concluded in his head.

FEET DON'T FAIL ME NOW

Without delay, they continue walking into the dimly lit nearly vacant parking garage. It was easy to see the garage had not been maintained, in fact, the ticket booth looked as if no one has been inside it for years. The two tall rectangular shaped glass windows have been broken out and walking by you could smell a foul odor coming through. Possibly a dead rodent of some sort, but they continued walking on an incline up the ramp. Considering the man of gold had yet to pull his pistol back out on him, Tim figures if he can beat him to the punch he will have a greater chance of getting away with his life. "Hey, what do you want from me man? Tim says, talking through his teeth as he stops abruptly cocking his head to the side staring the man down. The gunman gets so close to Tim's face that he can smell his stale cigarette laden breath. All of a sudden the man displays a grin on his face. "I see punks like you all the time. Bet you ran away didn't you? Tim decides there's no point going any further up the ramp. He looks over the man's shoulder as if he saw someone coming the man turns to look and Bam! Tim hits him with an overhand right hook directly in the eye. Tim bolts running zig-zag toward the bottom of the garage toward the opening. The man stumbles back against the wall with his left hand covering his left eye. He reaches into his pants, pulls out the gun with his right hand, fires aimlessly hoping to hit Tim but instead the bullet enters into the side of an old green truck. He squeezes the gold plated trigger again, then breaks into a sprint going after Tim. This time the bullet breezes past Tim's head, you hear it clang against the blue metal dumpster across the street. So instead of running out into the street he makes a sharp left in the garage. Then began crouching down as he ran so he would be at windshield level of the parked cars. At this point, the gold gunman is shooting recklessly trying his best to put a hole in Tim. In spite of this, Tim makes it up the ramp, squats down below the window seal of red sedan where he thought he could not be seen. Then without notice Boom! There's a loud crash! The window of the red car is shot out, the glass falls like rain all over Tim. His hands raise up by default trying to cover himself from the glass that is shattering above his head. Nonetheless, a large piece of glass cut the back of his head, he falls to his knees, then attempts crawling down the ramp to get to the exit. It was pointless to scream for help in this part of the city he thought plus making any noise would only attract more attention from his attacker. Momentarily, he thought this can't be real, this had to be a horrible nightmare! But this was no dream, this was all happening in real time. Just as he was crawling to the exit, suddenly the gunman appeared hovering over him. He looks right into the barrel of the gun. Bleeding lightly from his head, covered in sweat Tim sits on his butt defeated letting out a sigh. This was the end of his run, "Get up" the man said yoking Tim up by the collar, gun in hand poking him in the back with it. "You really wanna make me kill you, don't you?" After bringing him to his feet, he shoves his shoulder with his hand forcefully causing him to walk toward the exit of the garage. By this time, the few people that were outside had disappeared. They leave the garage and enter through the red double doors of the casino.

GOLDEN OPPORTUNITY

Once past the weather-beaten red double doors inside you're greeted by the overwhelming smell of cigarette smoke amongst other illegal substances burning in the air. The casino floor is spacious, crammed with cheap furniture along with outdated decor. Dirty wallpaper hugs the walls, with posters of upcoming performances which has long since passed. Dim red lights dangle from the ceiling. The once plush red carpet is now virtually black showing only accents of the red that once existed. In any event, they continue past several pool tables with rips, tears and stains on the felt. Oddly enough, none of the few patrons noticed the blood dripping from Tim's head along with the gun nuzzled in the small of his back. They near the elevator where there is a small wooden stage, a scrawny little man is doing a horrible rendition of Michael Jackson's song "Beat it". The man dipped in gold put his gun back into his pants, once on the elevator, he presses the button for the 13th floor. The man pulls up his shirt flashing the piece "Am I gonna have to use this? Are you feeling brave again?" Tim looks down at the floor, disheartened "Nah, I'm good". Letting his shirt flap back over the gun, "Good, let's go". The doors open they go down the dark hallway to room 1317 the door is already cracked open; they go inside. "Gold! Did you get another one? You sure know how to spot em" a man in a Kango hat with pork chop side burns laughs. The unidentified man's name is revealed, or nickname at least, he pushes Tim hard in the back, prompting him to take a seat on the tattered faux leather couch. There were two other boys Tim's age on the couch watching boxing on the TV when he walked in the room. They both lock their eyes on him sizing him up and down. "All I know is that I'm not sharing my work," said one of the boys arrogantly. "I'm saying though ain't we got enough people working already?" Tim is wondering what type of work this guy is referring to, becoming anxious all again. He's tired, bleeding, hungry and apparently in the wrong place at the wrong time. Gold heard the question while in the kitchen; he comes back with a pre-wrapped sandwich tosses it on Tim's lap. "Here, eat this, you gonna need it". Walks over to the boy who asked the question then took out his gun and hit him with all his might across the mouth with the butt of the gun. "You know better than to question me by now don't you?" The momentum of the hit swung the boys head hard to the right, so hard, in fact, you could see blood along with two teeth spew out of his mouth onto the floor. The boy falls from the couch onto the floor in pain, nearly unconscious. Tim just looks on in disbelief as Gold comes to sit on the edge of the ripped up coach looking directly at Tim. "Guess what? It's your lucky day young blood, I have a golden opportunity for you, aren't you excited?" He says sarcastically. "Yeah, see this is how it's gonna work, I'm gonna give you some packages and you're gonna deliver them. Simple right?" Tim gives him the evil eye and then focuses on the TV. Gold goes up to the TV turns it off, then walks back directly in front of Tim, who is seated on the couch coming face to face with him. "Am I gonna have to make another example in here today? Tim leans back in the couch with his arms folded. "Man, I just want to go home, this whole situation is crazy". Gold disappears for a few moments and returns with a small package, drops it in Tim's lap. "Don't open this, I'm going to tell you exactly where to take it and who to give it to" Tim looks down at the package then pushes it to the other seat cushion. "Hey, can I go to the bathroom to clean myself up? I am bleeding you know!" Gold pauses, then displays a halfhearted smile showing his gold teeth. "Be my guest" points to the bathroom. Once inside, Tim gags at the mind boggling smell of urine. The bathroom was hardly fit to use, but at least he was alone to think better yet pray to God Almighty for help. Looking in the cloudy mirror, he begins washing his face with water and the dirty soap bar scrubbing the now dried blood off. In a quiet voice, he says, "Our Father which art in heaven, hallowed be thy name, thy kingdom come, thy will be done on earth as it is in heaven...Lord that's pretty much all I can remember right now. I wish I knew more, but I need your help. First off forgive me for anything that I've done wrong, I didn't mean it, but you already know my life has been crazy and tonight is the worst ever!" Out of nowhere a loud pounding on the door is heard "Hey, hurry it up in there! You can't jump from the 13th-floor dummy!" Gold says sarcastically then walks away. "Ok God, I'm not even gonna pretend like I"m gonna be able to be perfect if you get me out of this but I'll do the best I can though. I remember Pastor Ron saying you've helped him out thousands of times, he always says he's not perfect. So maybe you can do the same for me?" He cuts the water off, sits down on the toilet stool deciding to let his face air dry as opposed to using the dirty towel on the rack. With his head down, shoulders sunken in, and eyes closed for about a minute his racing heartbeat begins to slow down. He starts to feel a great sense of unwavering peace as he utters a quote that he forgot he knew. "For God has NOT given me the spirit of fear but of power love and a sound mind". He keeps repeating it over and over and over. Without notice, Gold kicks the door open to the small bathroom with so much force Tim thought he was going to get hit with it. Eyes open jolted but not afraid he continues saying the verse as he gets up. "Boy, what's wrong with you? Get outta here!" Gold screams, grabbing him by the shoulders shoving him out the bathroom back into the living room. Tim continues to mumble heading back into the living room; he takes his seat back on the couch. The TV is back on, and the news is on "In the news tonight, a teenage girl has been reported missing in the 1500 block of Grand Ave in Clarksville. Let's go there now we have Stephen Jones on standby at the location" the female reporter says as the camera cuts to Stephen, the reporter on the scene. He's standing outside Stacy's house, there are police cars all around, and almost the whole block is outside in front of her house trying to see what's going on. "Ramona, were live here outside the home of Stacy Wilson, who was reported missing earlier tonight. There was an anonymous tip called in metro police indicating they saw two men shove the young girl into a black car around 10 or 11 pm. So far, there are no leads we did try to speak to the sister of the missing girl, but she declined to speak". They show a clip of Monique with her back turned arguing with someone on the phone. When the reporter approaches her, she shoves him then storms into the house. "We were able, however, to speak with a few of her classmates Rick & Marshall". The boys are seen gathered one on each side of the reporter on the front lawn. "Thanks fellas for speaking with us, had she mentioned anyone wanting to harm her?" The guys both look at each other, then into the camera as if they were hoping that where ever Tim was he would see this broadcast. They hoped that Tim would suspect that Darius was behind this as they thought. Marshall takes a deep breath, then spoke. "We'll honestly speaking, I'm sure this was an act of jealousy by someone we all probably know" then they immediately walk away from the reporter in different directions. "There you have it, Ramona, let's hope for the best, back to you". He says as he signals the cameraman to stop rolling. Tim's body becomes totally limp as he sinks his back into the couch. He felt as if his entire heart had sunk into his chest he's in total despair. He covers his face with both hands, lays his head in the upward position against the couch. After a minute, it was like he had a great revelation, drops his hands. "I gotta get outta here, I bet Darius had something to do with this, I'm gonna kill him," he says to himself. He quickly transitions from hopeless to being determined more than ever to break free so he can get back to find Stacy. Meanwhile Gold along with one of his workers are at the table smoking cigarettes, chopping up a big brick of what could only be cocaine into tiny chunks and placing them into bags. Unbeknownst to them Detective Morales along with a team of police were now in the parking garage investigating the shooting called in earlier. Detective Morales is walking around then stoops down to pick up a shell case off the ground. "I count about five shell casings so far; I want you guys to lock this whole area down right now! It's always something going on in this area. I wish they would just shut this eyesore down once and for all" he says rising back to his feet pointing in the direction of the hotel with his cup of coffee in hand. Walking back toward the entrance of the parking garage, he stops Officer Davis, places his left arm on his right shoulder. "Hey, you know it's been awhile since we've taken a look at this hotel. I feel it's time for a shakedown, what do you think? You never know our trigger-happy gunman may just be dumb enough to be inside". Officer Davis shrugs his shoulders "In this area, I wouldn't be surprised, I'll make the call for backup" he gets on his walkie-talkie as they head toward the casino front door. "Ok, guys let's get all doors covered. No one in, no one out!" Davis switches the channel to connect with police headquarters.

BET ON BLUE

Meanwhile, back at the police headquarters located 3 miles away from the casino, a gum-chewing red haired lady at the dispatch desk receives the call. "Dispatch," she says rolling her eyes, taking a deep breath. "This is Davis, calling in for immediate assistance. There's been multiple gunshots fired at the ShoGun Casino located 1516 Chalfont Boulevard. Requesting all available units at once for a sting operation" he says while pacing in front of the doors. Just then, a man and a woman come stumbling out the casino doors they appeared to be drunk. "Hey, hold it right there!" he shouted. "Griggs! Keep them over on the other side of the street for now. I don't want anybody inside to know we're out here" he says sternly pointing his handheld receiver toward the area he wanted Officer Griggs to go. Less than 3 minutes later a caravan of at least 30 police vehicles quietly advance down the boulevard. A motorcade of vans, patty wagons, cars, motorcycles the whole brigade was in full force with no lights or sirens visible. It's now 2:35 in the morning as the vehicles draw closer to the location, a few passers-by look in amazement, knowing something big is about to go down. 2:38 AM the cavalry arrives at the front door of the hotel. Morales comes to the curb to greet the Captain they began walking back to the front doors. "Sir, I think we should have men lined up to the left and to the right of the building. I need men in the back in case anyone tries to escape. Ok, we're going to do a complete shakedown floor by floor, were looking for drugs primarily, but I'm sure we'll find some perps with warrants as well. Hey, I'm hoping the shooter is crazy enough to be in there too". The captain nods, the other officers remained in their vehicles waiting for the official word. He then turns around holding up his right hand and motions with his pointer finger for them to come.

Almost simultaneously dozens of officers dressed in black riot gear, night sticks, shields exit their respective vehicles and meet at the door. The captain goes back to Morales, lifting up his hat rubbing his fingers through his salt and pepper sprinkled hair. "Morales, my men, are here and ready. This doesn't appear this is going to be a big score in my opinion, just a bunch of low-level bit players if you ask me. Frankly speaking, we both know I don't like you, but lucky for you, Chief likes you. But make no mistake about it, if this turns out to be a waste of time, money, and my sleep, you'll be on desk duty till you retire! Is that clear?" Morales looking around at all the manpower at his disposal then looks the captain dead in the eye. "I understand sir and with all due respect you can save that seat for right-hand man Wilson, unlike him I always get my man. Let's do this!" There is a mob of police at the red double doors, hyped up and ready for action. On the count of 3 they rush into the casino onto the main floor like a swarm of bees that are protecting the queen bee from danger. People are completely caught off guard as most are under the influence of some substance or the other, preventing them to even consider running. People are being thrust up against the walls, leaned over pool tables, and over the bar as well. Everyone is being frisked and patted down with little to no resistance. At the same time, Gold has ordered his worker Bruno to make a delivery in the casino lobby. The casino was Gold's official drug house he worked out a deal with the owner to allow him to sell inside the casino for a percentage of the take. A call would be made to the room and the runners would deliver the package in the lobby all day and all night. Gold didn't want to pay his workers so he would get runaways, put them to work in exchange for food and shelter. "Bruno, take this to Jimmy V over at the roulette table near the mountain bar," Gold says as he hits him in the gut with the mid-size package walking him to the door. "Come right back too!" he says harshly. Bruno is not the one for resistance his motto is "go along to get along" so while he's extremely sleepy, he drags himself down the dim hallway to the elevator like his every usual routine. Typically, as the elevator approaches you can hear a lot of noise and commotion from the people inside but this time it was unusually quiet. Bruno was so tired he was unalarmed by the silence. Once on the bottom floor the doors open, an officer points his gun in Bruno's direction and yells "put your hands up now!" Notwithstanding, if Bruno was sleepy before, his eyes were wide open now, he went straight to panic mode, pressing the 13 floor and the door close button in one motion. The officers start running toward the elevator, but it was too late to open the door. Morales saw what happened "I need a team of 6 to take the stairs on the west end, we've got a runner! There's no way to tell what floor he's stopping, on darn it" his said on his radio, resting his hands on his hips looking at the broken arrow above the elevator. Griggs makes his way over to Morales waiting for instruction. "Follow me" they head over to the check-in counter where Rojan the manager is completely hysterical. They go behind the counter to gain access to the hotel computer system. "Rojan, how many rooms are occupied tonight? Pull up all the guests you have in this shack you call a hotel now! Better yet, just give me the password? Rojan stutters, shakes his head, backing away from the computer "I, I, can't do that! Why are you harassing my customers like this? I know my rights" Morales gets on the computer pushing buttons to no avail looks over at Rojan "Oh, so you're a law student now eh? Funny, I thought you were just a scumbag who allows drugs to be bought and sold at your hotel and get a percentage. Somehow, I had you all wrong tisk, tisk. Well, I know a little about the law myself, how bout I charge you personally for every bag of dope plus any other illegal substance I find in here tonight?" Rojan adjusts his collar, clears his throat and nervously answers "you can't do that." Morales comes over to Rojan "Do you want to actually find out?" Rojan quickly thinks about that question carefully then utters, "5575". Morales returns back to the computer keypad enters the code then glances over and gives Rojan a sarcastic smile. "Thanks for your cooperation, now show me the list, I want the name of everyone in this hotel. "Rojan takes control of the keyboard reluctantly scrolling down the list of names scanning the check in dates. As he's scrolling Morales notices, Raven Jones has been checked in for the last 2 years according to the screen. Morales puts his finger on the screen "Hey, hold up right there, this Jones guy has been checked in April of 1993 how is this possible?" As he scrolls the mouse down the entire list, check for other persons with extended stays. Rojan shakes his head pretending to be amazed by the findings in the systems. "Well, what's the deal with this?" Morales says urgently. Rojan shrugs his shoulders and extends his arms wide "Who knows? It's just an error, relax, you know how these old computers get" as he walks away to the corner of the counter. "I highly doubt it, Griggs, I think we found a key player in room 1317. Radio in for a background on Raven Jones ASAP. Let's get to the 13th floor as a precaution now!" He walks from the behind the check-in counter towards the elevator rounds up 8 officers to accompany him as they file in the elevator headed to the 13th floor. At this point, Bruno has made it back to the room panicking and out of breath, he bangs on the door hard and fast. "Hey fool, why you banging on the door like you're the police?" Gold says angrily. "That's just the thing, the police are here!" once inside, he goes to the kitchen to grab a glass of water. Gold follows into the kitchen "Say what?" he slaps the glass of water from Bruno's hands so he can finish telling him what's going on. "You say the police are here and you got time to drink water? Are they on this floor?" he questions Bruno as he's running to the table, picking up as much dope as he can find so he can flush the toilet. He prompts the others to get up and do the same the problem is there are 100 bricks to dispense of and one toilet. "Aw man, this is unbelievable! We're gonna have to start throwing these out the window, everybody hurry up" he screams. The doors of the elevator open, the officer's exit, but congregate in front of the elevator. Just then, a call comes through on Morales radio "Yes, we have a Raven Jones in our system. Numerous priors for drug possession, assault and a few charges of kidnapping" the female voice says. "Ok, there you have it, were going in now!" Morales says quietly as he points for the men to go to the right side of the hallway to room 1317. They storm down the hall, one officer with a shield kicks the door in catching everyone in motion then. Luckily, Tim was in the back bedroom alone, gathering up the drugs out the closet when he heard the door blast open. He throws all the remaining bricks on the bed and squeezes into the small entrance to the hot water heater area and places the panel back. The police make the arrest, gather all of the drugs, money and finds the 9mm gun that matches the shell casings outside. Even with all their searching they never suspected or looked at the small area where the water heater was in the closet. Two hours had gone by Tim had dozed off figuring the area should be cleared, he quietly took the panel door down and came out. The place was completely ransacked, he stepped over heaps of trash, bottles, cans, the place was wrecked worse than before. He looked out onto the balcony and the bathroom window to see if any cops were still around. The coast was finally looking clear to exit the room, Tim peeked his head out into the hallway looking first to the left and then right. With no one in sight, he bolted for the stairs. Needless to say, he was ecstatic to be free from this place, he sprinted and jumped down the steps in the back stairwell until he got to the bottom. Pushing open the door to the back alley where the morning sun hit his face just as bright as when he defeated Darius at school. "Thank you, God, I'm finally free!" Tim was ecstatic, but the reality was there was still so much that he needs to handle once he got back home.

ROAD KILL

Coincidentally, at the same time Tim was enduring the worst night of his life there trouble was brewing for Sunny and her friend Patty. As Robinson went looking for Tim, Sunny, and her friend decided to go out for drinks at Lucy's Bar & Grille. A small dive bar located in Clarksville that all the locals go to for cheap drinks and great Caribbean food. The place was jam-packed tonight, but Sunny and her friend managed to find two seats at the bar L-shaped bar. Reggae music is playing in the background, people are dancing, laughing, having a good time as is the norm. "Girl, I'm telling you, you need to cut your losses and get out of there, get all the money you can and move on! There's nothing else to think about" Patty said while bopping her head to the music. Sunny glances at Patty briefly, then signaled over to the male bartender "Um, let me get a long island ice tea, Matter fact let me get two! I need to relax!" as they're both people watching at the bar. "Hey, Mr. Bartender can you ring me up for 5 long islands? If I gotta to listen to her talk me to death, I need to be relaxed" Patty says as they both burst out in laughter. "So anyway girl, what you gonna do?" The slim male bartender brings two drinks over and places, napkins in place before setting down the drinks. "It sounds like you ladies are having a rough night so I made them extra strong," he says with a flirtatious smile on his face. Patty winks at the bartender, then picks up her glass extending it toward Sunny gesturing to make a toast. Sunny hesitates but decides to put her glass up against her glass anyway. "What exactly are we toasting to?" Sunny says, looking confused, Patty responds sharply "To the boyfriend that you meet tonight, hopefully" she belts out, they both share in another laugh. After hours of drinking it's now one thirty in the morning, the same time Tim was held up at ShoGun in New

Franklin. The bartender comes over with a wash rag cleaning the inside of a glass looks at both ladies equally. "You know, I didn't ring you up for all those long islands in advance because I said to myself. There's no way you'll be able to finish 2 of them much less 5! Those are the strongest drinks I make here, ya'll have proven me wrong!" he said, shaking his head in astonishment. By this time both Sunny and Patty are entirely wasted, Sunny could barely keep her head off the bar. After hearing this, she tries to come back to life to show him she can handle her liquor. She attempts to get up but falls down hard on her butt, a man in a pinstripe suit, with a feather in his hat helps her back to her feet. He calls the bartender over after he gets her limp body back on the bar stool, she's only upright because her back is against the man's belly for support. He yells at the bartender "Yo, these girls are wasted! Why did you keep serving them like a fool? Get them some water!" he says angrily. The bartender looks as if he's unaware the ladies are intoxicated brings them two large glasses of water. "Look bro, these are grown women, they ask for it, I supply it, next time you babysit for them." He said as he walked to the other end of the bar to finish making a drink for another patron. "Man, I should beat the living daylights outta that dude," he says to Sunny, who is barely conscious. He holds their heads back one at a time giving them water to drink along with splashing a little on both of their faces. "Hey, what are you doing" yells Sunny after feeling the water dribble on her blouse. "Who are you? Are you tryna take advantage of me? Get your hands off!" She screams. The man is embarrassed by the scene she is causing as all eyes begin peer at him with concern. So without further ado he backs away looking to avoid being accused of anything foul. "Look, I was only tryna help, you ought to be thankful, good luck getting home!" the mystery man says as he disappears. The lights in the bar come up, signaling it was almost time to go "last call for alcohol" the DJ says as he starts playing a slow jam. Patty grabs her purse off the bar, with slurred speech, swaying back and forth "Sunny, let's get outta here" they both stagger out of the bar to the parking lot. They both manage to enter Patty's car, she sits in the front driver seat resting her head on the steering wheel. Minutes later a man comes to the driver side window, knocks on the glass, it startles them. "I don't think you gonna be able to drive, let me call you a cab." Patty opens her eyes "get away from my car!" she yells putting the keys in the ignition. Then backs up recklessly into 3 cars that were lined up and just misses two people standing next to the cars. She zooms out the parking lot into traffic not stopping or looking once. She's flying down Central St near CLP, cars are pulling over to the side because of her erratic driving to avoid getting hit. All of a sudden, Sunny comes to her senses after being shaken around in the car, notices Patty has nodded out, and they're headed straight for a pole "Hey! Patty wake up" she tries to steer the wheel, but it's too late, they run straight smack into a huge oak tree. Within minutes of the crash the man in the pinstripe suit who tried to help them at the bar, notices the back headlights of a car push forward into the tree. So naturally he stops to see what happened. He gets out and runs up to the door to see if he can help the drivers, but it's too late the drivers are both deceased.

TURNING OVER

During the same stretch of time, Tim was praying and planning for his heroic escape from Gold in New Franklin coupled with Sunny's untimely demise. It's 12 midnight and Stacy is enduring a dilemma of her own as she has yet to return home to her dad. Darius and three of his flunkies are driving around looking for a place to stop to determine what they plan to do with Stacy. Tamir is in the passenger seat looking over at Darius, who is behind the wheel " Ok, now, what exactly are we gonna do with her?" Darius bangs both of his hands against the steering wheel "man, don't be asking me no questions! I don't know!" he says angrily. Tamir looks out the window and mumbles under his breath, but loud enough to be heard "then why you get me involved?" Stacy, who is in the back seat with her hands tied behind her back yells "Tamir, are you serious right now? I can't believe you're going along with this, I thought we were friends!" With tears in her eyes as she attempts to lean forward in the seat but is pushed back by one of her handlers named Rico. Darius shoves Tamir in the shoulder with his right hand with such force he bumps his head on the window. Tamir holding his head with one hand screams "What are you doing? Are you crazy?" Darius cracks a devilish smile "Maybe, now don't get soft on me punk, this was just as much your idea as mine beside its' too late now!" He said as they near the entrance to an abandoned auto parts warehouse on Lake Willow. They pull into a vast open area near the edge of the water. The moon is the only source of light now that Darius has turned off the engine along with the headlights of the car. The other guys in the back seat exit first, they grab Stacy one has her legs the other has her arms. She's twisting and turning her body as well as screaming at the top of her lungs, hoping that someone would come to her rescue.

"Tamir don't do this! What's gotten into you?" she yells in total fear and disbelief. As it turns out, Tamir was having second thoughts so he walks away toward the edge of the water, squats down to grab and throws a few rocks into the water. At this moment, he realizes that he's gone well beyond the point of no return by bringing Stacy here. In his mind, he could not conceive a way out of this situation without unfavorable consequences. A myriad of questions flooded his brain at once. "How can I hurt Stacy? I love this girl. Why did hook with Darius to do this" he thought to himself. The guys struggle carrying Stacy toward the entrance of the warehouse. Meanwhile, Darius gathers rope, tape, and a butcher knife out the trunk. Then he notices Tamir isn't with the other guys. "Hey ya'll hold up!" he says carrying the items he gathered out the trunk over to the lake where Tamir is squatting down. "You better get it together! We bout to have a good time with ya home girl then guess what I'm gonna do? I'm gonna slice her up real good and she's going right over into that lake! Yeah, that's the plan, I finally figured it all out!" he says with a demented look on his face moving his head up and down in agreement with his decision. Tamir stands up, wipes the dirt off his hands onto his pants afterward he walks up close to Darius speaking in a low tone so the others could not hear what was being said. "Darius, man, we should just let her go, I mean we can't really kill this girl, come on that's crazy talk. I guess we could scare her a little bit, but, kill her? I just can't do it" as he turns to walk toward the car. Darius watches him walk away for about 10 feet, staring at him as if he has 3 heads, then quietly runs up to him turning him around with the knife against his neck. "It's either gonna be you or her or both, you decide right now punk! I should've known you were soft, but one thing for sure somebody's not leavin here alive! Now, are you in or are you out? You got one minute to decide" he says as the knife pricks under his chin starting a light dribble of blood to run down his neck. "Ok, ok, calm down I'm in, let's just do it and get out of here as soon as possible man." Darius lowers the knife from Tamir's neck they both turn walking in the direction of the warehouse. On the way Darius breaks his momentary silence "Hey, this is gonna be fun ain't it?" he said excitedly. In Tamir's head, he thought Darius is certified crazy and should've been put away in an asylum long ago. Meanwhile, Rico is still struggling to carry Stacy's arms he inadvertently drops her onto the concrete slab at the front door. There was a thick heavy chain in between the door handles preventing them from getting the door open without bolt cutters it appeared. "Yo, how we gonna get in there?" Rico said while kicking at the chain with all his might. They all take turns pulling and kicking at the chain to no avail. Darius is fed up with the failed attempts "there's gotta be another way inside this place" he says as he walks around the building looking for a side door or a window. "Dang, do I gotta think of everything for ya'll? Go look around!" he barks at them. Rice, as he was nicknamed due to that was all he had to eat most times growing up, finds an open window on the side of the building facing the lake. "D, check this out, this window's open, someone can climb in then open the door from the inside?" Darius and the others carry Stacy over to see the window Rice was referring to. "Ah, now you're thinking my friend, someone's ready to party I see," he says with a big Kool-aid smile on his face. "Let's do this, now who wants to go up? Ya'll looking scared? I can't believe I'm dealing with some scared wannabe gangstas, I'll go up myself" Without notice, Stacy is dropped on the ground a second time beneath the window. "Go grab me a few of those crates sitting over there so I can use to climb up, dumb head" referring to Rice. Rice lifts and carries the two large containers over and fixes them in the position so Darius can climb up. He carefully climbs up the crates, then hoists himself up to the window ledge. Once up there he is on his knees facing the inside of the window, he peers into the building but it's complete darkness. "Hey, I can't see nothing in here, we should've brought a flashlight! Man, I ain't going in here by myself, one of ya'll coming in here with me" as he looks down at the other guys. "So I guess Mr. tough guy ain't so tough, after all, huh?"

Says Tamir looking away. "What? You know what bring your butt up here now, you're coming in here too. Tamir backs up "Yo, grab that fool Rice, Rico you better act like you know, get him!" They grab him then force him back over to the crates, the guys stand behind, watching him as he goes up the ladder to join Darius on the ledge. "Hey, buddy old pal great to see you up here, the weather sure is nice. Well, looks like we're goin down together. Let's go on the count of three" they swing their legs toward the inward part of the window seal. "Darius, we have no idea what's down there! Why I gotta go with you?" Tamir is cut off in mid-sentence as Darius pushes him off the ledge, the momentum of the push caused Darius to lose balance so he falls as well. "Ahhhh," they both screamed for what seemed like 30 seconds each, turns out it was about a 10-foot drop onto an old tire pressing machine. Darius fell backward, hitting his head on a rusted metal tire rod that pierced through the back of his head. Tamir falls inches away on the flat end of the table, his leg is broken in 2 places. Rico and Rice hear the loud crash inside, they start yelling their names, hoping to hear some signs of life. After no response, they decide it's only one way to get inside the building now. They both run to the car, leaving Stacy on the side of the building, they decide to ram the front door in. Rico turns the car around, heads back about a 1000 feet, then floors it toward the front door getting up to 70 miles per hour. They hit the door with such great impact it blasts the doors open but pummels right into the 10-foot high rack. The frame falls onto the roof of the car smashing the roof completely down on Rico and Rice, who were both crushed to death. Nearby Tamir is losing a lot of blood and can't move from off the table, he passes out. Finally, Stacy is able to get back to her feet by pressing her back against the wall of the building. Hands still tied she begins walking toward the road where so she can be seen. Meanwhile, Robinson is in his car driving back from his sister Camina's house, he had hoped Tim went there for the night. In route, he notices a girl staggering toward the side of the road with her hands bound in the back of her. Slowing down, he sees its Stacy he immediately stops the car hops out and says "Hey, what in the world happened to you?" whips out his pocket knife to cut the ropes. She bursts out in tears, throwing her arms around his neck. "Thank you, thank you, thank you! You have no idea what I've been through tonight". She is squeezing and hugging Robinson tightly, he embraces her in his arms "your safe now, it's gonna be okay" as he takes off his jacket and wraps around her shoulders.

HOME

Back in New Franklin, Tim is rapidly heading west up Chalfont Blvd as the Sun is peeking its head out in the midst of the gray clouds. Ironically, there are only a few people on the Boulevard this morning. He continues his almost walk, run pace for nearly 2 miles toward the bus station. Then all of a sudden, two guys dressed in all black with hoodies over their head are coming toward him. They looked suspicious, mainly because they kept looking back nervously as if someone was looking for them. They began walking faster and faster toward him, one guy reaches into the left pocket of his jacket. Meanwhile, creeping up the street was an undercover police cruiser with a blue light on top. Tim kept walking with his eyes intently focused on the two men wearing hoodies coming his direction, so much so he didn't notice the unmarked car. Ultimately, he figured Gold described him to these guys and here they are doing his dirty work. With that in mind, he starts taking long, deep breaths hyping himself up to execute a swift yet vicious attack then take off for the bus station. Within himself he reasoned and said "Enough is enough, I'm not going out like a punk! I'm gonna take these dudes out and when I get my hands on Darius, it's lights out". Beyond his control, his fist balled up on their own as his would-be attackers near a few hundred feet. Unexpectedly, a loud siren goes off in addition to a blue light flashing as the unmarked car rushes up to the curb stopping abruptly. Two plain clothes officers dart out the vehicle chasing after the men at full speed. Tim is caught off guard and moves quickly into the doorway of a vacant pawn shop. The men take off running like track stars while sprinting one man inadvertently tosses a brown bag inches away from Tim's feet. Apparently neither officer noticed or cared what was in the bag as they continued the chase. So he pokes his head out far enough to see the police are still in hot pursuit. Quickly he slides his left foot on top of the brown bag, bringing it closer to him. Naturally, he was curious as to the bag's contents, as he picks it up, he notices it's kind of heavy. He unravels the medium-sized brown paper bag to look inside. To his surprise, it was a Glock 38 mm handgun with a gold handle. At that moment, his heart sank deep into his chest at the realization that this could've been his last day alive. He tosses the bag in the corner but stuffs the gun in his pants. Shaking his head up and down talking out loud to himself. "Yeah, this is just what I need right here." He makes his way to the bus station heads down the steps toward the ticket counter but stops in front of the gift shop across from the ticket booth. He looks around then set his eyes on a black shirt that read "New Franklin" in white letters. An unusual time to buy a souvenir for most, but there was no immediate plan of returning to the city in his mind. At the ticket counter, he purchases a ticket back to Clarksville. Afterward, he takes a seat on the metal bench thinking about where Stacy could be, along with how he plans to take Darius out once they meet again. The bus arrives at 10:56 Am he hops on board and sleeps the entire ride back, but wakes up as the bus driver pumped his brakes jerking the passengers forward by mistake. Tim is anxious to get off as he waits for 10 people in front of him to exit the bus. Inside the station, he checks the bus schedule back to his part of town. After seeing it was an hour wait for the next bus, he looks out the front door noticing that cabs are waiting. Once outside, a cab is pulling up which Tim signals over to him. It just so happens, the bus driver he saw the night he left town is walking slowly toward the cab with her coworker Retha. The taxi driver brings the car to a complete stop next to the curb. "Girl, ain't that the boy you thought was running away?" Retha says point directly at Tim. The bus driver takes a hard look "hmm, I think you're right" she says. Retha says, "I figured it was, it looks like him alright to me, well let's go we can't be late for work." Tim pulls on the door handle as the bus driver rests her right hand on the top of the door to prevent him from open it fully. He was surprised to see her and tried to yank it, but after he had looked in her eyes, he decided against it. "Young man, whatever you do, have mercy on others just as God has had mercy on you," she said as she removed her arm from the top of the door then closed it. The older white haired male taxi driver says, "Where to? Youngin" in a raspy voice. "Take me to 1535 Grand Ave," he said then the driver makes a left out the parking area headed toward Stacy's house. During the ride, he got excited to see familiar houses and stores from around the way. He gazed out the window digesting all that's happened to him over the last three days. Then he thought about what the driver said, but quickly blocked it out his mind turning his focus on using that gun on Darius. He wanted to stop by Stacy's house in hopes that Monique would be able to give him some clues on his quest to find her. Upon arrival at Stacy's house, he is shocked to see his dad's Mercedes parked out front. Robinson had taken Stacy to the hospital after the ordeal to make sure she was okay. Afterward, while dropping her off, he stayed to talk with her father who was slowly regaining his ability to speak. The driver turns back, putting his arm over the seat. "Ok, that'll be 10 big ones" Tim is puzzled trying to figure out why his dad was there. He opens the door then without looking at the man or his money gives him a $40. The old man's eyes pop out looking at the money, Tim gets out the car "Hey" the old man yells "what about your change?" Tim doesn't even turn around "keep the change," he said almost in a fog, he goes to the front steps where he can see inside the open screen door. He opens the door, sees his dad, Stacy, her father and Monique all sitting in the living room on the mustard color sectional. Robinson and Stacy's faces light up like they have just seen as a ghost. Robinson and Stacy run to Tim at the same time almost competing for the first embrace which Stacy wins. He's excited and relieved to see them both as well. Meanwhile, Monique is sitting with her arms folded on the couch, turning her body in the opposite direction to avoid making eye contact. She starts crying silently without anyone noticing her. After what seemed like forever, Stacy loosens her grip around his waist. Without delay, Robinson comes forward with tears of joy falling from his eyes and gives Tim a bear hug. Tim allows his body to lay limp with a somewhat embarrassed grin on his face granting his dad to enjoy the moment. However, when he is swung around the gun falls to the ground and goes off. "Boom" everybody screams apparently taken back from the blast along with the sight of the gun. No one was injured, but Tim scrambles to get the gun, which fell by the front window. He grabs the gun, turns around slowly noticing all eyes are on him. There is complete silence, Robinson puts his hands up "Tim, son, what's going on? What do you plan to do with that son" he says inching closer with caution. Tim feels the tension in the room waving the gun in his hand "Hey, everybody calm down, I'm not gonna hurt anyone here. I've got some unfinished business to handle" Monique jumps off the couch, rushes up to his face. "You wanna kill Darius with that gun don't you? Don't you? Well, you're too late! This is all your fault, I hate you!" She brushes past him storming out the front door. Tim stands there in disbelief yet cracks a smile puts the gun down on the living room table. Then he looks back at everyone "Dad, Stacy, I guess I won't be needing this after all". They all come together for a group hug. "I love you Dad," he says his dad responds still in tears "I love you too son." All of a sudden, the door opens abruptly Monique comes in crying hysterically sees the gun on the living table, takes it without being noticed and fires a shot! Someone is shot!

To be continued

Thanks for reading visit www.timmknight.com to get chapter reveals of part 2